C000198075

A *Swing* at *Love*

Harper & Caroline
BLISS

OTHER HARPER BLISS BOOKS
Once Upon a Princess (with Clare Lydon)
Crazy for You
Love Without Limits
No Other Love
Water Under Bridges
This Foreign Affair
Everything Between Us
Beneath the Surface
No Strings Attached
The French Kissing Series
In the Distance There Is Light
The Road to You
Far from the World We Know
Seasons of Love
Release the Stars
Once in a Lifetime
At the Water's Edge

To all the lady-loving Lady Golfers.

PREFACE

Dear Reader,

Before you start this book, I feel as though I have some expectation management to do. You'd be hard-pressed to find a Harper Bliss book without a steamy scene... until now. After a long discussion, Caroline and I have decided to make this golf romance a 'sweet' romance. My claim that it wouldn't be a proper Harper Bliss book without a sex scene was rejected by Caroline's argument that this isn't a Harper Bliss book, it's a 'Harper & Caroline Bliss book'. And she was right. Caroline and I wrote this book together. It was a shared effort across the board and, in the end, I'm glad we chose to write *A Swing at Love* this way. More than anything else, it's a heart-warming, cosy village romance and for this particular co-write, it felt very natural to just fade to black. All of that being said, I hope you enjoy our joint effort. For us, married-to-each-other writers, it was a struggle at times, but no divorce lawyers were called and we're very proud of the end result.

Harper Bliss

CHAPTER ONE

Diane's ankle twisted as the heel of her shoe caught in between two cobbles. She steadied herself on a parked car and gave her foot a tentative turn to determine if there was any serious damage. A light pain jabbed through her ankle but it was nothing unbearable.

She continued her walk to the clubhouse at a more careful pace. She was already late, but being one minute less late wasn't worth ending up in a wheelchair for. The bloody high heels were a couple of inches taller than Diane was used to wearing. But they matched her maroon evening gown so well, or so the lady in the shop had told her, rightly seeing her as easy prey.

She climbed the steps to the main entrance and hurried towards the cloakroom.

"Good evening, Mrs Thompson," the attendant greeted her.

"Has the presentation started yet?" Diane asked as she took off her coat and handed it over.

"I'm afraid it has." The girl smiled apologetically.

Diane made her way to the clubhouse's main function area.

She could already hear the booming voice of the club's president. She reached the room and slipped in at the back.

The sofas and armchairs that usually clustered around the elegant coffee tables had been pushed to the side. Behind them the large bay windows overlooked the putting green and eighteenth hole, now shrouded in dusk. Several elaborate flower arrangements adorned the ledge in front of the windows. The decorating committee had obviously spared no expense for the event.

Diane craned her neck to try and see the front of the room, where Stephen, the Royal Tynebury Golf Club's president, was giving his speech to open the new season and introduce the new members, but even her higher heels didn't make Diane tall enough to see above the heads in front of her.

"In conclusion, I wish you all the best season you've ever had," Stephen's voice came over the speakers, "and without further ado, please enjoy the wonderful food and drinks we have lined up for you tonight."

The crowd erupted in applause and, on cue, waiters brought out trays of Champagne from the large oak bar.

Diane made her way through the crowd, greeting people and making small talk as she progressed. She kept her eyes peeled for her ex-husband and spotted him towards the front of the room, his arm around the shoulders of *Debbie*. In Diane's mind that name always came out in a childish tone, probably because Debbie was about the same age as Diane's own son.

"I think her boobs look bigger, she must have had them done over the winter," a familiar voice whispered in Diane's ear from behind.

Diane smiled as she turned around to face her friend, Isabelle. "Not what I was looking at, but now that you mention it." Diane opened her arms and embraced Isabelle. "It's so good to see you. When did you get back from Florida?"

"Two days ago," Isabelle replied. "I would have called you,

but the transition from Floridian sunshine to British drizzle was rough." She shivered. "Anyway, catch me up on the gossip. Did anything juicy happen while I was away?"

Diane laughed. "I'm afraid I have to disappoint you. I haven't been here much, what with the course being closed a lot because of the weather."

Isabelle squinted at Diane. "Your absence wouldn't have anything to do with the fact that young Debbie there has been taking lessons and visiting the driving range more often—probably to prove she's worthy of her new member status?"

"Let's just say that it didn't help my motivation to spend time at the driving range."

A waiter stopped in front of them. "Mrs Thompson, Mrs Avery, can I offer you a glass of Champagne?"

Both women eagerly grabbed a glass.

"Speaking of new members," Diane said, "where are Rob and Matthew? I only got here at the end of the speech so didn't get to see Matthew being introduced."

Isabelle shook her head. "He wasn't accepted. They're not here tonight."

"What?" Diane exclaimed. "Why? What happened?"

Isabelle sighed. "They weren't given a reason. I haven't been able to corner our dear president yet to grill him about it, but trust me, I'll get to him before the night is over."

"Would you like me to make some enquiries?" Diane asked. "I know at least one other person on the admissions committee."

"No, not yet," Isabelle answered. "I want to see what pretext he gives me first. Of course, he won't tell me openly that this place is still so stuck in the fifties that the same-sex spouse of one of their lifelong members is less acceptable than the class-less bimbo your ex now calls his wife. No offence."

"Oh, none taken." Diane smiled at her friend. She knew Isabelle was probably much more affected by her son-in-law's

3

rejection than she was willing to let on tonight. "It's so good to have you back. Let's set up a date this week to play a round. I need to get back in shape before the Ladies' trip next month. You can show me again how wintering in the Florida sun does wonders for your game."

"Diane." A male voice came from behind her.

Diane cringed and turned around to face her ex-husband. "Lawrence." She offered a cheek for him to peck, grateful at least that he'd had the courtesy to come and greet her alone. "How are you?" She had to admit he still looked quite dashing, especially in his tuxedo.

"Jolly good, my dear. And yourself?"

Diane tried to keep her tone neutral as she replied, "I'm very well, thanks."

An awkward silence followed. Diane and Lawrence's divorce had been finalised five years ago, but they had not yet reached the stage where small talk came easily.

Diane hoped Isabelle would say something to break the tension, but when she turned her head to give her a pointed look, she found her friend had scarpered off somewhere, abandoning her to face Lawrence alone.

Diane turned back towards him. "Have you seen Timothy recently?" At least their son should be a safe topic.

"He and Lucy came over for dinner the other night. Debbie made shepherd's pie. You know that's still his favourite."

Diane fought to suppress an eye-roll. "How lovely." No way did *Debbie* cook a shepherd's pie as good as hers. "I hear Debbie is now a full member of the club. You must be delighted."

"Ah, yes," Lawrence beamed. "Very happy, quite right. She's been working hard, trying to get certified so she can start playing on the course."

Diane could see Debbie moving through the crowd, making her way towards Lawrence. "Excuse me, would you? I need to powder my nose before we get ushered into the dining room."

4

She turned around and walked towards the exit into the hall. Attempting a civil conversation with her ex was one thing, but having to be polite to his new wife was not on the cards yet.

On her way out, Diane deposited her empty glass on the tray of a passing waiter and grabbed a new one. More bubbles were required to fight back the bad taste she got in her mouth every time she saw Lawrence and Debbie together.

She took her glass into the ladies' changing room, hoping to find a quiet spot to gather herself before having to sit down for the dinner, which was bound to last too long. It was the same thing every year.

She sat on a stool in front of a vanity unit and checked her make-up in the mirror. She rifled through her small evening purse to find her lipstick.

The door to the dressing room opened. A short-haired woman Diane didn't know walked in and looked around uncertainly. She must be one of the new members.

"Are you looking for the bathroom?" Diane asked. "It's past those lockers on the right, then through the first door."

"Thank you," the woman replied with a smile. "I haven't quite got the lay of the land yet." She walked in the direction Diane had indicated and disappeared into the bathroom.

Diane turned back to face her image in the mirror. She applied a new coat of lipstick, checked her eyeliner was still as it should be, and stood. The pain in her ankle had all but disappeared—probably thanks to the two glasses of Champagne she'd consumed. She took one last look in the full-length mirror—her shoes did indeed match her gown perfectly, she couldn't take issue with the salesgirl's taste. Debbie might have almost thirty years on her, but youth could never make up for elegance. At least that was the mantra Diane was going to stick to tonight.

She pulled back her shoulders and headed out towards the function room as the bell was rung to call people to dinner.

5

CHAPTER TWO

Tamsin hurried out of the ladies' room and into the grand dining room. Long tables were set with folded name cards next to the plates. Good. She wouldn't have to scour for a seat—all she'd have to manage was to find her assigned spot. A wooden lectern displayed the seating plan. A crowd huddled around it, so Tamsin waited and cast her glance over her new place of employment. This evening might be just a dinner, but to Tamsin it was as nerve-racking as the first day on a new job. So many unknown people, so many names and faces to put together and remember.

The crowd at the lectern had dispersed and Tamsin scanned the large piece of paper for her name. Now all she had to do was locate the table. A few people were already sitting there. They probably all knew each other—but mingling with the members was part of her job.

She walked over to her table and spotted the friendly lady who had shown her where the bathroom was earlier. She smiled and found her seat, right next to her.

"Hi," the woman said, extending her hand, "Diane Thompson."

"Tamsin Foxley." Tamsin shook the woman's hand. Her grip was firm. Her blue-eyed gaze on Tamsin unwavering.

"Lovely to meet you, Tamsin," Diane said. "You must be one of the new members." She smiled apologetically. "I arrived late so I missed the introductions."

"I'm the new club pro, actually," Tamsin said. "I'll be replacing Darren when he leaves in a few weeks."

"Oh, how wonderful," Diane said, turning towards her more. "My game's always a bit rusty after the winter break. I must book some lessons." Diane pushed her glasses up her nose.

Tamsin felt a little under-dressed next to her, but she'd never really been one to dress up.

"Of course. That would be lovely," Tamsin said.

"Diane, how are you?" An elderly man had approached and put his hands briefly on Diane's shoulders. "I believe you're stuck with me for the evening." He pulled back the chair on the other side of Diane.

"Have you met our new pro, Reg?" Diane said.

Tamsin repeated the motions she'd gone through many a time since she'd arrived at the club: shaking hands, smiling broadly, and replying to chit-chat.

Reg kept Diane engaged in conversation for a while. Tamsin was relieved she'd been seated next to someone as welcoming as Diane. If the opening dinners of her previous club were anything to go by, they'd be stuck with each other for a few hours.

Tamsin picked up the menu card that stood in front of her plate. Smoked salmon as a starter and steak for mains. The number of times she'd had a similar meal at a golf club. She smiled inwardly. Golfs clubs were not known for grand innovations and any change—even to the menu—was always slow.

"Which club were you with before?" Diane had turned to her again. She gave Tamsin a warm smile.

"Chalstone," Tamsin said, a pang of regret shooting through her.

"Any particular reason you left?" Diane inquired.

"I was in dire need of a change of scenery." She sent Diane a wide smile. Tamsin was eager to keep the real reason she left— or rather, had been forced to leave—under wraps.

Diane nodded thoughtfully. "Do you live nearby?" She took a sip of the white wine that had just been poured.

"I found a place on the outskirts of the village," Tamsin said. She looked at the glass in front of her but left it alone for now. She'd had two glasses of Champagne already and, unlike most of the other guests, she wasn't here to relax tonight. "Very quiet and green." Tamsin had fallen in love with the small cottage, which was modest, but stretched her rental budget considerably nonetheless. Even though Tynebury was a good number of miles from London, it was still a commutable distance to the capital.

"Welcome to the club *and* the village, then." Diane lifted her glass.

Tamsin mirrored her action. They clinked rims. "Are you joining the Ladies' trip to Portugal next month?" Tamsin asked.

"Oh, yes." The skin around Diane's eyes crinkled when she smiled. "I'm looking forward to it greatly. Winter has been long. I need a good dose of vitamin D."

"And an equally good dose of golf, I hope." Tamsin attempted a joke.

"That goes without saying." Diane drank again, then set her glass down. "I do miss playing during the off season." Her gaze on Tamsin was kind. "I should book those lessons before the trip, by the way. I hope your calendar's not too full yet."

"I'm sure I can squeeze you in." Tamsin's calendar was still very empty. She wanted—needed—to teach as many classes as she possibly could.

Diane's eyes locked on a woman strutting past their table.

When she glanced back at Tamsin, the kindness in her eyes had disappeared.

"That *woman*," Diane said with utter contempt in her voice. She straightened her spine. "I'm sorry. I shouldn't have said that."

"Debbie?" Tamsin inquired. She'd been introduced to Debbie earlier, who had promptly also inquired about lessons.

"It's just so unfair." Diane leaned in Tamsin's direction. Tamsin caught a whiff of her flowery perfume. "Since you'll be working here, you might as well learn about the medieval politics of this club." She shook her head. "My good friend Isabelle's gay son-in-law has been refused membership, while my ex-husband's trollop of a wife has been accepted," she whispered. "Sadly this club has not yet entered the twenty-first century, I can assure you of that."

Tamsin momentarily stiffened at the mention of the word *gay*. She reached for her glass of wine so she had some time to regroup. "That's simply appalling."

"It is, and I'll do everything I can to make sure Matthew gets accepted next year. What is this? The middle ages?"

"I sure hope not." Tamsin was distracted by a bunch of waiting staff milling about. The starters were being served. With that, Reg engaged Diane in conversation again, and Tamsin was left in welcome silence to ponder the information she'd just received.

———

Tamsin scanned the improvised dance floor. She wasn't much of a dancer and she preferred leaning against the bar, letting her gaze wander. Dinner had gone well, largely thanks to her welcoming neighbour. More people had come up to her after dinner to introduce themselves and enquire about lessons. She knew from experience, however, that members of these old, traditional golf clubs were always very welcoming at first, brimming with courtesy and warm smiles, but it was only the thinnest veneer that hid the true nature of some.

A man sidled up to her. "How are you holding up?" She recognised him as Lionel, who had sat at the far end of her table, which, Diane had revealed near the end of the meal, was dubbed the 'singles' table'.

"Just fine, thanks."

Lionel had loosened his tie and his eyes were glazed over.

Tamsin took a small step away, not that she considered him in any condition to take a subtle hint.

"You'll find us a lovely, civilised bunch." He all but slurred his words.

Yeah right. Like the lot at my previous club.

"I'm sure you all are." Tamsin had little choice but to oblige him.

"I hear you're renting the Andersons' cottage," Lionel said. "Is it just you there or do you have a husband and some kids running around?"

How quickly word spread in villages—and clubs—like this. Of course, the Andersons were members here as well. Any newcomer would have tongues wagging. She knew how this worked.

"Just me and Bramble, my dog," she said. Bramble had acclimatised to the cottage and its surroundings instantly. Tamsin adored the cottage but knew she would need a little longer to adapt to everything else.

Lionel took a step closer again. "We'll have to make sure you don't get too lonely over there then." Lionel tried a smile but the corners of his mouth seemed too lazy to quirk all the way up.

Tamsin thought it best to not dignify that with an answer. She looked at the dance floor again. Diane was chatting to a woman at the edge of the bopping crowd. She didn't seem like much of a dancer either. Of all the people who had inquired about lessons tonight, Tamsin looked forward to teaching Diane the most. They'd spent the most time together, so it was only logical. She didn't much look forward to teaching Debbie —what had Diane called her again. A trollop? Tamsin snickered inwardly, careful not to show any outward signs of her glee, lest Lionel believed she was actually enjoying their conversation.

Diane must have felt Tamsin's gaze on her because she looked in her direction and gave her a wave. Her gaze lingered, then meandered to the person next to Tamsin. She rolled her eyes.

Emboldened by Diane's small display of sympathy at being stuck with a drunken Lionel, Tamsin said, "Please excuse me." She turned away from him, only to be accosted as soon as she rounded the corner of the bar by another member in dire need of golf lessons.

CHAPTER THREE

"Damn it," Diane muttered as she watched her ball fly over the green and end up in the bunker behind it.

Isabelle was using her new special binoculars to measure the distance to the hole. "They're the newest, most accurate model," she'd said, proudly showing them off to Diane on the first hole. "And so much cheaper in the US. If you want I can ask Ted to bring you some, he's going back in a couple of weeks to take care of some business."

Diane had politely declined the offer. She was a firm believer in instinct and her own eyes. All these new technological innovations were lost on her. These days people even had watches that told them the distance to the hole.

Now, looking at where her ball had ended up, she was starting to think that a little help from technology would not be such a bad thing.

Isabelle finally decided on which club to use. She set up in front of her ball and took a calm and elegant swing at it. They both followed the ball with their eyes as it flew through the air until it landed on the green, rolled for a few seconds, and ended up two yards from the hole.

"Nice shot," Diane said. "Did you do anything besides play while you were in Florida?"

Isabelle grinned at her. "Not really, no. I've told you many times, you should consider doing the same. We should go over together soon and you can look at condos. Then we can spend the winter together in the sun."

"It does sound more appealing every time you mention it," Diane mused. "But as long as I'm still working, I don't feel I can be away for that long."

"Oh, come on," Isabelle exclaimed. "You only go into the office three days a week as it is. Your loyal employees keep the place running without you there. And, I know you're a techno-phobe, but there's this thing called the internet. Even Florida's connected to it. You could work remotely."

They had reached the green. "I'll think about it," Diane said. "Now let me focus on getting this ball out of that bloody bunker."

After they had finished the hole, they saw they had caught up to the foursome in front of them. They sat on the wooden bench next to the tee as they waited their turn.

"Can you believe how slow they are?" Isabelle pointed at the septuagenarians playing ahead of them. "They're probably still hungover from the dinner on Saturday. Did you see how drunk Barry Ferguson was? I saw him almost fall on his face on the way to the car park."

Diane chuckled. "Most of those old codgers don't usually stay out that late. You can't blame them for having a jolly time."

They sat in silence for a while and turned their faces towards the sun, making the most of its unexpected appearance. The trees were not showing signs of new leaves yet but the air smelled of the possibility of spring for the first time that year.

"Have you booked any lessons yet with the new pro?" Isabelle asked.

"I haven't, but I plan to do so soon," Diane replied. "I was sitting next to her on Saturday; she seems very nice."

"She does, doesn't she?" Isabelle said. "Did she happen to mention why she left Chalstone?" Her tone was conspiratorial.

"She said she needed a change." Diane looked at Isabelle. "Why? Do you know more?"

"I probably shouldn't be saying this, as it's only a rumour I heard from Ted's friend, who'd heard it from someone else." She paused. "Apparently—and again, this is just a rumour—she had a fling with the daughter of Chalstone's president. That didn't go down well, as you can probably imagine. Plus, said daughter is only about twenty, according to my source, so they said she was taking advantage of the girl. Miss Foxley's contract was therefore not renewed and she was asked to leave."

Diane sat in stunned silence for a moment. Then she said, "How sure are you of this?" Diane knew enough about golf to not be surprised that the new RTGC golf professional was sapphically inclined, but Tamsin had seemed completely decent and genuine, not the type to take advantage of anyone.

"As I said, I only have third or fourth-hand knowledge." Isabelle shrugged. "Could be someone failed to improve their handicap sufficiently after lessons with her and decided to discredit her out of spite."

The older gentlemen had moved on. Diane and Isabelle both hit their drives onto the fairway. As they were walking towards their balls, Isabelle said, "In any case, I for one would be very happy to have another out LGBT person at the club. Rob and Matthew sometimes feel so out of place. Maybe she can help Matthew get his membership accepted, finally."

———

After they'd finished their round, Isabelle had rushed off, claiming the slow play had made her late for an appointment.

Diane was in the warehouse where the golf bags were stored, cleaning the mud from her clubs. She straightened when the door opened and Tamsin walked in.

"Hello Diane," she said, "are you starting or finishing?"

"I just played a round with Isabelle," Diane replied. "My first one since before Christmas, can you believe it?"

"Is that Mrs Avery?" Tamsin asked. "I'm not familiar with all the names yet."

"Yes, that's her."

"How did it go, after your long break?"

"Not very well." Diane laughed. "Let's just say you'll be seeing me on your teaching schedule sooner rather than later. If it's not completely booked out yet, that is."

Tamsin took her phone out of her pocket. She tapped the screen a few times, then held it out for Diane to look at. "As you can see, my schedule for the next few days is still pretty empty. Darren has been encouraging his pupils to give me a try, and many have approached me, but I guess they'll only actually start coming once he's gone."

"Well," Diane said resolutely, "I for one don't want to wait. New year, new start and all that." Diane thought she had spotted the name Deborah Stamp in Wednesday's calendar and decided not to take any chances. "Are you free Thursday afternoon, say, at three o'clock?"

Tamsin checked her phone. "Not anymore." She smiled at Diane. "Thank you."

"Did you have a nice time at the party Saturday night?"

"I did, but I went home quite early. It's rather tiring meeting all those new people, trying to remember everyone's name."

"I can imagine," Diane said. "Especially when most of us had a few too many to drink. I saw you managed to fend off Lionel's advances." Diane winked.

Tamsin chuckled. "Yes, I did."

"Not your type, is he?" Diane asked before she could stop herself.

"Eh, no, not really." Tamsin blushed at the question.

"I'm sorry," Diane said, placing her hand on Tamsin's arm. "I'm always saying things I shouldn't."

"That's all right," Tamsin said. "Don't worry about it." Her mouth opened and she looked like she might say something more, but then decided against it.

An awkward silence followed. Diane realised her hand was still on Tamsin's arm, and quickly retracted it.

"Well," Tamsin said, "I should let you get on with your cleaning. I want everything spic and span for Thursday." She wagged her finger and gave Diane a stern look, before breaking into a wide smile.

Diane laughed and gave a salute. "Yes, Ma'am."

"See you then." Tamsin walked towards the back of the warehouse, where the pro's office was located.

Diane's gaze followed her and lingered on the spot where Tamsin had disappeared from view behind a row of stored bags.

Diane was intrigued by the new teacher. She had an easy manner with people and an engaging personality—as far as Diane could tell after only a couple of encounters. These were probably prerequisites for someone in Tamsin's profession. Nevertheless, Diane felt like they would get along. Despite what Isabelle had told her on the course, Tamsin definitely didn't seem like someone who would act inappropriately with anyone. Diane vowed to do her best to make sure Tamsin was welcomed at the RTGC.

CHAPTER FOUR

"How about you show me a swing," Tamsin said. "See how far you can hit the ball."

Diane looked like a natural in her golf outfit, as if she'd been doing this all her life. She probably had. She wore a bright orange polo shirt and a pair of navy-blue trousers. Her golf bag was perched on an electric cart.

Tamsin had taught a lesson to 'the trollop' the day before and, although she'd been dressed in similar garments, Debbie didn't come near the effortless elegance of Diane.

Diane selected a seven iron and positioned herself for her swing. Tamsin studied her movement as she hit the ball.

"Can you do that a few more times, please?" she asked.

Diane didn't say anything; she just focused on hitting the balls. Tamsin had looked up her profile on the club's internal website, as she did with everyone who booked a lesson, and she had learned that Diane Thompson's handicap was a very respectable thirteen.

"I'm impressed," Tamsin said. "You get a really good length with that seven iron." She took a step closer. "Do you mind if I show you a little trick to get your direction more consistent?"

19

"That's what the lesson is for, isn't it?" Diane grinned, her eyes sparkling as she did.

"Indeed." Tamsin stood behind Diane. This was always a little bit awkward with new pupils, but she was a teacher and, sometimes, there was no other way to demonstrate something. She put her hands on Diane's arms and pulled them up slightly so her hands held the club a little higher. "Can you feel how this straightens your legs?" Tamsin asked.

"Yes," Diane said.

Tamsin let go of her. "Keep that position." She crouched down to tee up a ball. "And try another swing."

Tamsin watched Diane's improved form. It was only the tiniest of changes, but they were what made the difference in golf.

"How did that feel?" she asked.

"Like I could hit a little better." Diane painted on a satisfied smile.

"You have a natural draw in your shots, which you should always take into account," Tamsin said.

Diane nodded. "I've missed many a hole-in-one because of it," she joked.

They worked on Diane's swing for the rest of the lesson. Tamsin hadn't taught many lessons at her new club yet, but from the few pupils she'd had, Diane was definitely top of the class. She had a confidence about her that came from having played the game all of her life. Tamsin had also gleaned from the club's website that Diane had won quite a few club championships, although her winning streak had ended a few years ago.

When they came to the end of their lesson, Diane said, "I couldn't help but notice when you showed me your calendar the other day that you were due to have a lesson with Debbie Stamp."

"The woman of the *t-word*," Tamsin said, allowing herself

this inside joke with Diane—even though it was extremely unprofessional.

Diane nodded, her lips curved into a lopsided grin. "Do you think she's close to getting her handicap yet?"

Tamsin pursed her lips. "I think it'll be a while."

"Good." They walked to the clubhouse together. "Do you have time for a coffee?" Diane asked.

"When you inadvertently glanced at my calendar, you may have also seen that it's still quite empty," Tamsin said. "I have all the time in the world."

————

They sat by one of the large windows overlooking the putting green. Tamsin had chosen coffee, whereas Diane had claimed she deserved a glass of wine after her lesson.

"How long have you been a member here?" Tamsin asked.

"All my life," Diane said. "My parents were members." She narrowed her eyes. "I'm the one who got Lawrence in and what thanks do I get? Him ushering in his younger model." Diane took a sip of wine. "I'm sorry, you must think I'm still very bitter about the divorce, while I'm really not." She lifted a finger. "But I am still very much riled-up about Debbie being allowed to join. Not only because the committee decided against Matthew joining, but also because this club has always been a refuge for me. After my divorce, I came here a lot so that I could forget about the whole mess. For a while, Lawrence felt too guilty to show his face much, what with having turned into such an utter middle-aged cliché." Diane shrugged. "But now Debbie has invaded this part of my life as well, while all I want to do is pretend she doesn't exist."

"That must be hard." Tamsin wasn't new to pupils baring their soul to her. When you spent a lot of one-on-one time with someone, it happened quite naturally.

"It is what it is, of course." Diane leaned back in her chair and stared out of the window. "I've no choice but to accept it."

"If it's any consolation"—Tamsin leaned over the table —"from what I've seen, there's not much chance Debbie will ever become a great golfer."

"That *is* a consolation." Diane dragged her gaze away from the window. Her grey-blue eyes landed on Tamsin. "Thank you."

"This is strictly between us, of course," Tamsin whispered.

"Your secret's safe with me." Diane narrowed her eyes, as though she was going to say something else, but she must have thought twice about it, because silence fell between them.

"Can you put me in for another lesson for the same time next week?" Diane asked after a while.

"With great pleasure."

Diane gave her a wide smile. It reminded her about what Ellen had once said about Tamsin's. *Your smile can light up the darkest room.* For once in her life Tamsin had really—really— liked someone. She'd known the significant age gap between them wasn't ideal, and that their affair perhaps didn't stand a lot of chance, but that was for Ellen and her to figure out, not for Ellen's father to put a very offended stop to.

Maybe it was time she started dating again. Put the past well and truly behind her.

"Something on your mind?" Diane asked. "You look completely lost in thought."

"Just thinking about how to improve your game. Do you want to work on anything specific?"

"Well, I'd say let's get my handicap down, but it's been going up steadily for the past decade so I guess that's out of the question." Her gaze held Tamsin's for a split second. "A bit like my weight, actually." She belted out a brash, loud cackle of a laugh. "And, inevitably, my age." She reached for her wine glass again. "I'm turning fifty-five next year, in case you're wondering."

"Let me give you a dash of hope," Tamsin said. "I've been doing this job for a while now, and I've seen many women in their fifties improve their handicap. Not by a great margin, but it can be done. The downward spiral doesn't have to continue." Tamsin wanted to add that Diane looked in great shape for her age, but she didn't want to sound patronising.

"I'm suddenly very glad that Darren's retiring," Diane said. "I get nothing but good news from you."

"You're the one who has to put in the work." Tamsin used her stern coach's voice.

"I practically live at this club. I have more meals here than I do at my own home." She tapped a fingertip against her glass. "And more drinks as well." Another one of her smiles.

"Are you retired?" Tamsin figured they'd reached a stage where she could ask a more personal question.

"No, I still work part-time." Diane twirled the stem of her wineglass between her fingers. "I go to the office most mornings. I own an accountancy firm. I can't really see myself actually retiring any time soon. I can hardly play golf all the time."

"A handicap's something that can always be worked on."

Diane shook her head. "A lot of my friends at this club fill their days with golf and bridge, but I get a lot of satisfaction from going to work—and earning my own money."

"I'm actually looking for a new accountant. Someone closer to where I live," Tamsin said.

"Well, then look no further." Diane grabbed her purse and dug through it. She unearthed a business card and handed it to Tamsin. "Call me any time."

"I'll take you up on that." For the first time since she'd moved to Tynebury, looking for a much-needed fresh start, Tamsin had the feeling she was on the verge of making a good friend.

CHAPTER FIVE

"Mum, we have some news," Timothy said at dinner on Friday. He and Lucy were sitting across from Diane, eating the shepherd's pie she had prepared.

He had unexpectedly called Diane a few days earlier to ask if they could come over and spend the night. Usually she had to plead and beg for Tim and Lucy to make it down to Tynebury for a visit. Not that she blamed them; they had a full and exciting life in London.

Diane's heart started beating a little faster at Timothy's words. Could it be...?

"We're expecting a baby," he continued. "It's a little earlier than we had planned, but hey ho, these things happen." The smile he sent Lucy as he was talking belied the reluctance of his words.

"Oh Tim, Lucy," Diane said, her heart bursting with joy. "I'm so happy for you both." She stood up and walked around the table to give Lucy a hug, her eyes welling up. "How far along are you?"

"Three months," Lucy said. "I'm just about starting to show."

"You look radiant," Diane looked Lucy up and down. "I should have known something was up when Tim called to say you wanted to come over."

"Oh Mum," Tim said, taking Diane into his arms for a hug. "You know we'll be down here all the time once the baby's here —free babysitting and all that." He released Diane from his embrace and gave her a wide grin.

"I wouldn't have it any other way," Diane said. "This calls for some Champagne, don't you think? A small glass won't hurt you, Lucy. Goodness knows I had the occasional tipple when I was pregnant with this one here"—she pointed at Tim—"and he seems to have turned out just fine."

Diane hurried to the cellar to fetch a bottle from the wine fridge. She took a moment to steady herself. She was going to be a grandmother. She could hardly believe it.

She returned to the dining room, stopping by the kitchen to pick up some flutes.

"Here, darling," she said, handing the bottle to Timothy. "You do the honours."

He popped the cork and poured out three glasses.

Diane picked hers up and held it in front of her. "To you, Lucy, for giving me my first grandchild. May there be many more to come."

"Mother," Timothy said laughing, "let's not get ahead of ourselves. We'll start with one and see how that goes."

"All right, all right," Diane conceded.

They drank from their Champagne and sat back down at the table.

"Have you told your father yet?" Diane asked.

"No," Timothy said. "We wanted to tell you first. But we're going over there tomorrow to give him the news."

"I hope your news doesn't give Debbie any ideas," Diane blurted.

Timothy and Lucy guffawed.

"Mum," he said, clearly amused by her comment.

"Sorry, darling. I shouldn't say things like that." Diane looked at him apologetically. "But she *is* about the same age as you. Her biological clock must be manifesting itself."

"I know," Timothy said. "I still find it hard to wrap my head around sometimes. Can you imagine Dad having a kid with Debbie? He or she would be younger than ours." He looked quite appalled at the whole idea.

"I would rather not think about that, dear," Diane said. "But I have to hand it to your father, he was always very good with you when you were a baby. He definitely did his share of the night-time feeds and nappy changing." She paused. "That doesn't mean I can imagine him doing it all again now. Anyway, I don't think you need to worry. Debbie doesn't seem like the type who'd want to sacrifice her figure, not even for a child." She winked at her son.

———

After they had finished dessert, Lucy went to bed in Timothy's old bedroom which now served as a guest room. She was tired from the journey down and, Diane suspected, she wanted to give Timothy some alone time with his mother.

Diane came into the living room carrying a teapot and a couple of cups on a tray. She put the tray down on the low table in front of the sofa.

"Would you like a biscuit with this?" she asked him as she poured them each a cup. "I think I have some in the pantry."

"This is fine, Mum. I'm so full from dinner. You know I can never stop myself having seconds—or thirds—when you make your shepherd's pie. It's the best." He smiled at her.

Diane did an internal dance of triumph at her small culinary victory over Debbie.

"It's so nice to have you down. I really hope you meant it when you said you'd be here more often once the baby comes."

"I promise"—Timothy put his hand on his heart solemnly —"that we will come and see you all the time. You'll wish we stayed away more."

They drank their tea in silence.

"Have you never thought of trying to find someone new?" Timothy asked after a while.

Diane almost spat out the tea in her mouth, so unexpected was this question coming from her son. She swallowed and replied, "I have thought about it, of course. It would be nice to meet someone to share things with." She paused. In the immediate wake of the divorce Diane had harboured many thoughts of finding a dashing, successful man she could show off to spite Lawrence. After a while the thought of spiting Lawrence had faded and Diane had simply hoped for a companion, dashing or not.

"The thing is," Diane said, "I don't even know how I would go about meeting someone."

"Aren't there any eligible bachelors at the club?" Timothy asked. "How about Lionel?" He sent her a cheeky smile.

Diane picked up a cushion from the sofa and threw it at him. "Don't be ridiculous."

"But, seriously, Mum," Timothy said. "If you want to meet someone, there are ways. Have you tried making yourself a Tinder profile?"

Diane scoffed. "That's even more ridiculous than the idea of dating Lionel."

"I'm serious. Most of your time is occupied either by work or the golf club. You'll never meet someone new if you don't move out of your comfort zone. If internet dating is not your thing, how about going on an organised trip, or a cruise? There must be dozens of travel companies who cater to people in your exact situation. The grey pound is big these days." He grinned at her.

Diane waved off his suggestion. "I told Isabelle I might go to Florida with her next time she flies over. Maybe I can meet a rich American retiree when I'm there. And that's the end of this conversation."

Timothy picked up the teapot and refilled their cups.

"I *have* made a new friend," Diane said. "Or at least I think we're becoming friends. It's Tamsin, the new pro at the club."

"Oh yes," Timothy said. "Dad mentioned there was a new professional starting soon. How is she?"

"She's very nice," Diane replied, her lips expanding into a smile. "I took a lesson with her yesterday. I already feel like I'll be able to lower my handicap very soon."

"After one lesson?" Timothy looked slightly incredulous. "Now that would be efficient teaching."

"Anyway, I talked to her quite a bit at the season opening dinner." Diane chuckled. "Old Lionel tried to make a pass at her after dinner."

"Oh no, competition for you."

"Stop it," Diane said. "Anyway, from what I hear, she wouldn't be interested in Lionel, him being a man." She paused. "On a more serious note, have you spoken to Rob recently? He must be cut up that Matthew didn't get accepted to the club."

"Rob tried to call me a few days ago," Timothy said, "but I missed his call. I was thinking of going over tomorrow, since I'm in the area." He sighed. "That's really terrible. I know the club's old-fashioned and traditional and all that, but I didn't think it was that bad." He thought for a few seconds. "Is there anything we can do? Is there some kind of appeal procedure?"

"I don't think so," Diane said. "He'll probably need to wait until the next application period and try again. Which I'm not sure he'll do. Tynebury might have been Rob's home club since he was a child, but I wouldn't be surprised if they tried to find somewhere else that will accept them both, gay or not. And the RTGC really shouldn't drive away its younger members."

"Very true," Timothy said. He put down his cup on the tray and stood up. "On that note, I think I'll go see if Lucy has settled in. I'm pretty knackered."

Diane stood as well and embraced her son. "Sleep well, darling. Thank you for making me so happy tonight."

CHAPTER SIX

"How are things in the countryside?" Eve asked.

"Green," Tamsin said. "And spacious." To her sister, her move away from London had been rather abrupt. "Bramble loves it."

"How about you?" They sat on Eve's tiny balcony—if you could even call it that, enjoying what they could make out of the sunset in between the high-rise buildings.

"I'm getting used to it. The club's nice." Tamsin sipped from her gin and tonic. Eve always used Hendrick's gin and topped it off with an elaborately carved slice of cucumber. "I've given some lessons already. Darren, the old pro, will be retiring soon. It's all looking pretty good."

"Not much chance for love in a village like that, though." Eve and her husband James had helped move Tamsin's belongings from her tiny flat in Croydon, on the outskirts of London, to the cottage in Tynebury.

"You never know." Tamsin smiled at her sister. "We are many and we are everywhere these days."

"Is that why you came all the way to London to go on a date?"

"I came to London to see my sister," Tamsin said. "The date tomorrow is just... I don't know. Something I might as well try while I'm here."

"Thus proving my point," Eve said. "Tell me about this date, then. Is she of age?"

Tamsin shook her head. She guessed she deserved some snark from her sister. "She's in her late twenties." She fished her phone out of her pocket. "I'll show you a picture."

"Late twenties?" Eve rolled her eyes. "Are there no available lesbians in their late thirties? This is London, for crying out loud."

"Here." Tamsin ignored Eve's outcry. "Cute, right?" Andi's profile picture had immediately jumped out at Tamsin last week, when she'd been 'consulting' Tinder. She had long blonde hair, big brown eyes, and a constellation of adorable freckles on her nose.

"Late twenties," Eve repeated. "I don't think so. She looks to be more in her early twenties, perhaps even late teens."

"Don't be silly," Tamsin said.

"As if no one ever lies on their Tinder profile." Eve put her glass down. "You won't want to hear this, but in that picture, Andi is the spitting image of Ellen."

"So, I have a type. What's wrong with that?" Tamsin sipped from her drink to hide her agitation.

"I just think you'd have more chance at a successful relationship if you tried dating someone closer to your own age."

"James is ten years older than you," Tamsin said.

"Exactly. Ten, not twenty. It makes a world of difference."

"Andi's only ten years younger than me." Tamsin knew her sister meant well—she had to admit she didn't have the best relationship track record.

"So she says." Eve sighed. "And what if you miraculously hit it off? Are you going to do long-distance with a woman who's at a totally different stage in her life than you?"

"Hold your horses, Evie. It's just a first date."

"Do you want my honest opinion?" They were waiting for James to bring home a takeaway and were on their second drink.

"You're asking me now?" Tamsin grinned.

"I sometimes think you subconsciously choose women you don't really have a future with."

"Been watching Oprah again, have you?"

"I'm serious, Taz. You always date these twenty-somethings. But you seem to forget that you aren't in your twenties anymore. In fact, we'll both be forty soon."

"Don't remind me." Tamsin drank again.

"It's kind of a big thing for me as well."

"Why? You have everything to be a happy forty-year-old." Tamsin couldn't help but compare herself to her twin, but their lives had always been vastly different. And Tamsin had taken a big step when she'd decided to go for that job in Tynebury— and move away from the city.

Eve rolled her eyes again. "It's not about having things. It's about balance."

"And your point is?" Tamsin saw her sister as the very picture of balance.

"No one has it together all the time. Not even me."

"I didn't say you had, but you're pretty happy, aren't you? You don't have too many regrets?"

"I have a good life, but there's always room for improvement."

"Maybe you should move to the country. I know this cute little village about an hour and a half away from London. You have family there."

"And have James leave the city?" Eve shook her head.

"I'm not so sure," Tamsin said. "When he helped with the move, I could see some appreciation in his eyes for my new surroundings."

"Maybe for a weekend away."

"Quite a few people do the commute and what with all the working from home these days."

"He's forbidden to work from home. I already work from home." Eve grinned. "This is my territory!"

The intercom buzzed. "Speak of the devil." Eve rose. "He's probably forgotten his keys again." She headed inside to buzz in her husband.

Ten minutes later, the three of them sat huddled over plates of butter chicken and garlic naan. Tamsin had missed a good takeaway. She was lucky to find an open supermarket past 6PM in Tynebury.

"Your sister-in-law has a hot date tomorrow," Eve said, with obvious glee in her tone.

"It's just coffee," Tamsin said. She fought the urge to kick her sister in the shins underneath the table—she'd done plenty of that when they were younger.

"Coffee can go a long way," James said, in his typically amiable James way. Tamsin couldn't imagine her sister being with a nicer man.

"I'll keep you both posted," Tamsin said, even though she had no intention of doing so. She needed to meet Andi first.

———

Tamsin stared into her coffee cup. She and Andi seemed to have already run out of topics of conversation. The main reason, Tamsin realised, was that Andi didn't know the first thing about golf. The only thing she'd said about it, after Tamsin had told her what she did for a living, was, "Isn't that a sport for old farts?" Granted, the grin on her face when she'd said it had been adorable, but Tamsin needed a little more to work with than that.

Her sister's words rang in her ears. *We'll both be forty soon.*

"Have you seen the latest *Avengers* movie?" Andi asked, breaking the silence. "Maybe we can go see that."

Ellen had been more a rom-com kind of girl, eschewing superhero movies, for which Tamsin had been glad. What was she doing comparing Andi to Ellen, anyway? She shouldn't be looking for a replacement Ellen. She truly believed she hadn't been. She'd set the search parameters on Tinder so that no one younger than twenty-seven would show up. Ellen had been twenty-six. Tamsin inwardly cursed her own silliness—she'd only gone and fooled herself again.

"I'm not sure going to the movies is such a good idea, after all," Tamsin said.

"Oh," Andi said.

Tamsin wondered if that was genuine disappointment crossing her face or if she was just a good actress.

"Let a girl down easy, why don't you?" Andi offered a smile.

"Look, Andi, it's not you. From what I can tell, you're a lovely girl. But I just got out of something… rather painful. Perhaps I've put myself out there too soon." *And I'm twelve years older than you and live in Tynebury.* She hadn't been entirely honest in her Tinder profile. It still stated she lived in London. She hadn't had the heart to tell Andi that she'd recently moved to the countryside. The date was cringe-worthy enough as it was.

"I get it." Andi flipped her long hair back with a practiced gesture. "Maybe in a few months, eh?"

"Maybe." Tamsin gave her a wide smile. Next time she went on Tinder, if she ever did again, Tamsin would narrow her search to ensure any future dates lived closer to her new location. Not that she expected to find many women of her persuasion in a twenty-mile radius around Tynebury.

Tamsin rose and leaned over to kiss Andi on the cheek. "It was lovely to meet you," she said.

Andi didn't respond.

"Bye, then," Tamsin said, and exited the coffee shop. She hadn't picked it and, truth be told, she'd felt a little out of place among the hipsters with their MacBooks, manbuns, and trendy clothing.

Maybe she had reached *that* age, where she couldn't pass for someone ten years her junior any longer. Until she'd moved to Tynebury, Tamsin had dressed like the people in that coffee shop, but her choice of what to wear had altered along with her change in location. An image of how Diane Thompson had been dressed at the golf club's opening dinner popped into her head. Whether she liked it or not, that was the crowd she was mingling with most these days.

Maybe her taste in women was changing as well.

Tamsin walked through the streets of London a while longer before picking up her car at her sister's and driving back to Tynebury—back home.

CHAPTER SEVEN

"Ladies, if you could all grab your suitcase from the bus." Suzanna, the Lady Captain of RTGC yelled at the group of chattering ladies assembled in front of the entrance to Hotel do Golf in Vilamoura. "Leave your golf bags, as these will be driven straight to the club ready for us this afternoon."

Diane waited her turn until she could grab her small suitcase from the bus's luggage compartment. She didn't envy Suzanna her leadership position on this trip. They had only just flown out this morning and already she'd had to repeatedly yell instructions and recover a few women who had wandered off on the way to the boarding gate, as if she were herding a flock of wild sheep.

When everyone had retrieved their luggage they made their way into the hotel lobby.

"Maggie," Suzanna called. "You're with Judy, room 327. Here are your keys. Go up to your room to settle in, then meet us back here at noon for lunch."

"Diane and Isabelle," Suzanna turned to them. "Here are your keys, you're the only ones on the first floor. May I repeat what I wrote in my email: please try to keep the noise level to a minimum. We don't want a repeat of last year's trip to Spain, or I'll have to separate you." She eyed them with a stern look.

Diane and Isabelle kept a straight face. Last year's Ladies' trip to Spain had ended with them being reprimanded for laughing too loudly in their room, keeping their next-door neighbours awake well past their usual nine o'clock bedtime.

They burst out laughing when they were out of earshot in the lift.

"This is worse than being on a school trip," Isabelle said in between laughs.

"Suzanna's past career as a boarding school matron does reveal itself quite clearly on such occasions," Diane said.

They found their room and unpacked their suitcases. The trip was only four days long, but the room was too small to have two suitcases lying open on the floor.

"Do you think we were put in the smallest room as punishment?" Diane asked.

"At least we have separate beds," Isabelle answered. "If Suzanna really wanted to punish you, she would have given us a double. Ted tells me it's impossible to sleep next to me as I move around so much and kick him with my cold feet."

"I shall count my blessings then," Diane said.

———

After all the ladies had come back down from their rooms and gathered in the lobby, they had lunch on the terrace, which overlooked the golf course.

Diane sat at one of the tables waiting for the buffet line to shrink. She stretched her arms above her head and threw her head back. "Hmm." She gave a groan of satisfaction as she felt the heat warm her face.

"Is this seat taken?" a voice came from above. She looked up to find Tamsin towering over her.

"No, please sit so you get out of my sun." Diane smiled as Tamsin deposited a plate, filled with various salads and a few pieces of cured meat, on the table. "Not eating?"

"I am," Diane said. "Just letting the vultures grab their food first. I hate waiting in line."

"Queuing up is below Diane Thompson, is it?" Tamsin said playfully.

"Of course it is. Don't they know who I am?" Diane went along with the teasing.

"How's your room?" Tamsin asked. "I couldn't help but notice a hint of reprimand in Suzanna's tone when she was distributing the room keys."

"Oh, don't mind her. She enjoys treating middle-aged ladies like boarding school girls." Diane smirked. "Our room is tiny, but adequate. How about yours? Who did matron assign you to share with?"

Tamsin's lips expanded into a wide smile. "I have a room to myself. I suppose being the new girl has its perks. Or maybe she wants to keep some distance between teacher and pupils. This being more of a school trip in her mind." Tamsin's smile turned into a grin.

"Lucky you," Diane said.

"I've been looking forward to this trip very much," Tamsin said, gazing out at the view in front of them. "In my previous club they never organised these kinds of excursions. Beats teaching in the British drizzle."

"Then we will try to behave ourselves to make this trip pleasant for you in every way." Diane gave Tamsin what she hoped was an angelic smile. "Now if you'll excuse me, the crowds at the buffet have dispersed so it's my turn to go serve myself."

"Ladies," Tamsin shouted, "please grab whatever club you use for a low chip close to the green. You'll need three balls each."

They were gathered next to the practice green of the Vilamoura Golf Club. Everywhere Diane looked, the grass was manicured to perfection and every bunker seemed to have been freshly raked. The clubhouse walls were covered in bright pink blooming bougainvillea. It really was an idyllic spot to spend a few days.

Diane had her eight iron in her hand. This was a part of her game that was still pretty strong, so she hoped Tamsin would be organising some form of competition between the ladies.

"As you can see, I have lined up markers on this side of the practice green." Tamsin gestured towards the row of little flags about six feet apart from each other. "Choose one and then hit three chips towards the hole. When everybody is done, we'll all move to the next marker. After that we'll do the same thing with one ball, but you have to place the ball within three feet of the hole."

Several of the ladies with a higher handicap gasped and started protesting.

"Now, now," Tamsin said. "You get to practice beforehand; I'm not that mean." She smiled at them. "Every time you manage to get your ball in the target zone, you get a point. The person with the highest score at the end of it will get a drink at the bar tonight, on me."

Diane took a spot next to Isabelle at one end of the row. She hit the first practice ball and watched it end up just behind the hole.

"Nice shot, Diane," Tamsin shouted.

Diane played her next two shots in quick succession. The balls ended up on either side of the hole, but still a respectable distance from it.

She looked up to see if the others were finished. Most of

them were concentrating so hard that they were still only on their second ball.

Diane snickered.

"What are you laughing at?" Isabelle asked from behind her.

"They're all taking this so seriously," Diane whispered. "Look at everyone, it's like their life depends on getting this shot right. It's only a bloody practice shot for goodness sake."

"Or maybe they really want to impress our new teacher," Isabelle said, looking at Tamsin.

Diane also moved her gaze towards Tamsin. "That's probably it. The way a few of them came fluttering up to her to chat about inanities when we were having lunch, you'd have thought she was some hunky PGA Tour pro."

Tamsin was showing Maggie where to place her feet when she was lining up the ball. Tamsin's bright blue shorts showed off her toned calves. The short sleeves of her white RTGC embroidered polo shirt revealed quite impressive arms. Of course, it made sense that she would have an athletic figure. She was a sports professional after all. But there was something else about Tamsin that gave her the kind of charisma that both men and women alike were drawn to. Diane wasn't quite sure what it was. Maybe her boyish short hair. Although could the term *boyish* really be used to describe a forty-year-old's hairstyle?

Diane was woken from her reverie by Isabelle bumping into her shoulder. "Move over," Isabelle said, "time for the next station."

Diane hurried to pick up her balls from around the hole and made her way to the next marker. This time her balls all ended up a few feet past the hole. She cursed inwardly. She had better concentrate a little more if she wanted to be the one to earn that drink later.

CHAPTER EIGHT

"What can I get you, Diane?" Tamsin asked. It had been a long day of travel followed by the chipping and putting competitions and most of the ladies had retired for the night. Only Diane and Isabelle remained.

"This Portuguese wine is delicious," Diane said. "So I'll gladly have another one of these." She lifted her near-empty glass.

"Isabelle? Same again for you?" Tamsin asked.

"I wouldn't dare," Isabelle said. "I didn't earn it the way Diane did." She stretched her arms above her head. "I think I'll turn in. Long day and all that."

"That's Isabelle's way of saying she's feeling her age," Diane joked. "I'll be quiet as a mouse when I come up."

"I'll be right back." Tamsin headed to the bar to place her order.

While the bartender poured their drinks she glanced backwards and saw Isabelle kiss Diane on the cheek. Even saying a simple good night to each other was a chatty affair for these two.

"Here you go." Tamsin deposited Diane's fresh glass of wine on the table in front of her. "Do you mind if I sit?"

"I certainly don't want to drink my victory drink alone. What would be the point of that?"

Tamsin sat down opposite Diane and held up her glass. "To your chipping skills."

"Thank you." They clinked rims. "Do you have any other games in mind for tomorrow? I'd like to prepare myself psychologically."

"Please give the others a chance."

"I can't let you buy anyone else a drink now, can I?" Diane held her gaze, making Tamsin wonder how many of these glasses of wine she'd had.

"I can't discriminate, you know that." Tamsin played along.

Diane pursed her lips. "A contest automatically excludes discrimination, that's the beauty of it."

"You'll just have to do your best then." Tamsin sipped from the wine. It was, indeed, delicious. She let her head fall back. "It's great to be away for a few days."

"It is for me," Diane said. "For you, this is work, though."

"Teaching golf has never really felt like work to me. More like a dream come true." Tamsin counted her luck every single day—except that one day when her previous club had all but kicked her out.

"It's great when you love what you do," Diane mused.

"To me, there's nothing more important."

"You must come across a really annoying pupil sometimes, though?" Diane inquired.

"Well, there's this woman at my new club. Diane something." Tamsin winked.

"I hear she's a nightmare. So full of herself, and always wanting to win all the competitions, even the most insignificant ones." Diane glanced at Tamsin over the rim of her glass.

They both chuckled. It was hard for Tamsin to remember

when she'd last had a laugh like that, with someone who didn't take herself too seriously. Definitely not with Ellen, who was at an age where everything was deadly serious—especially seducing her golf teacher.

"Do you enjoy your job?" Tamsin asked, to get her mind off Ellen as quickly as possible.

"It's numbers all day every day, but I do genuinely enjoy it," Diane said, before taking a sip from her drink again. "Which reminds me, come by my office after this trip. I don't charge for an introductory visit."

"How nice of you." Tamsin had wanted to make an appointment but had hesitated because she'd be laying out her entire financial situation to one of her pupils. She wasn't sure she wanted to do that and had considered looking for an accountant who wasn't a member.

"Anyway, enough shop talk. For once, let's not talk about golf or the, admittedly, very fascinating secrets of accountancy," Diane said.

"Agreed." Tamsin nodded.

"If golf is your job, what do you do for relaxation?" Diane asked.

"Golf being my job, I don't need that much relaxation. There's nothing like being outside playing on a beautifully designed course. The green grass. The wind in my hair. Bird song."

"All of that might be true, but you must do things that are not golf-related."

Browse on Tinder. Go on dates with women I've no future with. "I have a passion for vintage furniture," she said, pushing thoughts of other women to the back of her mind. "It's one of the reasons I wanted to move to the countryside. To have room to work on some projects. My small flat in Croydon didn't really lend itself to it so I always had visit my dad up north if I wanted to work on something. Quite a hassle, although a good way to stay in touch with my father."

"Ah yes, city life and all its conveniences."

"My previous club was only a twenty minute drive from where I used to live, and I was out in nature all the time. Best of both worlds, really."

Diane nodded thoughtfully. "Why did you say you left your former club again?"

Tamsin tried to remember if she had said anything to Diane about that. She certainly wouldn't have divulged the real reason. "Sometimes you need a change."

"I guess you can't keep on teaching the same old people." Diane offered a supportive smile.

The golf world was a small one. It would only take one member-in-the-know at Chalstone to say too much and rumour would spread like wildfire—quite possibly, as rumours went, with a few salacious details added in the process.

"You might think the RTGC is homophobic, but if they really are, they'll have to fire me soon." *Oops.* Maybe Tamsin had partaken of the wine a bit too much herself. But Diane had given her an opening when she'd shown her outrage about Isabelle's son-in-law. Surely she must believe in equality.

Diane arched up an eyebrow. "So you're gay."

Tamsin gave a slight nod. "As is many a lady golfer." She found a joke always lightened the mood when she delivered the news.

Diane giggled. "I can't possibly imagine Chalstone fired you simply for being gay. That would be against the law."

"I wasn't fired, just encouraged to leave. And it was a little more complicated than that." Tamsin sighed. "Everyone knew I was a lesbian. I came out not long after I started, which is not a given in a traditional golf club." She took a sip of wine and noticed her glass was almost empty. "But I thought it was important to be honest, and it was." At least it gave Ellen the strength to come out, she thought.

"I wholeheartedly concur," Diane said, her lips drawn into a soft smile.

"Tell me truthfully." Tamsin leaned forward. "Have you heard any rumours about me?"

"How about I tell you all I know over another glass of wine? My shout."

Tamsin nodded eagerly. She wanted to know what was being said about her and Diane was the closest thing to a friend she had at her new club.

After Diane had presented her with another glass of wine, she slanted over the low table between them, and whispered, "One of the things I heard was that you might be a lesbian." Her glance skittered away from Tamsin's. "The other is that you got it on with the daughter of the club's president."

"I'm impressed by your sources." Tamsin hoped the smile on her lips wasn't too wry.

"Are you saying the rumours are true?" Diane's voice shot up a little.

"Ellen and I were in love. And she was twenty-six at the time. Hardly someone who can't make her own decisions." Tamsin knew she sounded defensive, but she was so sick of having to explain herself.

"Twenty-six," Diane said under her breath.

"The only unfortunate thing about our relationship was Ellen's father." Tamsin shook her head. "I wasn't a man and didn't come from enough money—I didn't pay an astronomical fee for the privilege of playing at the club; instead I got paid for teaching there." It wasn't as black and white as that—nothing was—but after a few glasses of wine Tamsin refused to see the grey areas.

"That must have been hard." Diane's eyes had found hers again. Her gaze was soft and almost comforting.

47

"According to my sister I don't do myself any favours by falling for women in their twenties." Tamsin furrowed her brow. "I hate to admit she's right, but..." She threw up her hands. "In this case, she just might be." She chuckled. What else was she going to do? And she wasn't still that hung up on Ellen. Deep down, perhaps she'd always known they didn't have much of a future, because Ellen still had so many mistakes to make, so many youthful adventures to have, while Tamsin was more than ready to settle down. "Thank you for not judging me," Tamsin said. "You've no idea how much that means to me."

"We only just met a few weeks ago," Diane said, "but you really don't strike me as the type to take advantage of someone's youth." She ran a finger over her chin.

"Then you already know me better than the president at my old club ever did."

CHAPTER NINE

Diane pondered Tamsin's last comment as she sipped her wine. She wanted to believe that Tamsin would not have acted inappropriately in any way. However, she couldn't help but be slightly taken aback by the age of Tamsin's previous love interest.

"Do you always fall for younger women?" Diane asked. "I don't mean to pry, and you don't have to answer if it makes you uncomfortable."

Tamsin stayed silent for a moment. Then she said, "I suppose I do tend to go for women who are younger than me. Looking at my dating history, I can hardly deny it." She gave Diane a rueful smile.

"Hm, interesting," Diane said. "Do you know why that is? Are you hoping their youth will rub off on you, or that your maturity will rub off on them?"

"Are you turning into a therapist?" Tamsin let out a chuckle. "I didn't know accountants were trained in psychology as well as numbers."

"I'm sorry, I shouldn't have asked," Diane said. "It's the wine catching up with me. I seem to lose sight of proper social boundaries when I've had a few glasses of vino." She held up her glass, which was close to empty. "Speaking of," she said, "can I get you another one?"

Tamsin immediately stood up. "It's my turn. Same again?"

"But—"

Tamsin held up her hand. "No arguments. But I will expect permission to ask you my own probing questions." She strode off towards the bar.

As before at the club, Diane found herself staring at Tamsin's retreating figure with more intent than expected. While she was waiting for the bartender to pour the drinks, Tamsin turned around and their eyes locked. The look on Tamsin's face was slightly mischievous—at least to Diane.

Tamsin returned with the two glasses and deposited one in front of Diane. "Here you go."

"Thank you," Diane said, holding up her glass for Tamsin to clink hers against. "I truly didn't mean to be so inquisitive before. I think I've been alone for so long now that I find other people's relationships and dating adventures much more interesting than I should."

"So you're just very nosy?" Tamsin said.

Diane nodded. "It's true. But I have an excuse. I'm going to be a grandmother soon, and a tendency to stick one's nose into everyone's business is kind of expected of grandmothers, wouldn't you agree?"

"Oh Diane, that's great news," Tamsin said. "Although you don't look nearly old enough to be a grandmother, so I don't think you can use that as an excuse for anything." Her lips were pulled into a wide grin.

"Thank you, I think," Diane said. "I'm very happy. Timothy only told me a few days ago. But, truth be told, I can't really associate the title of grandmother with myself just yet."

"So," Tamsin sat up a bit straighter, "now that we've

switched the conversation to you, it's my turn to ask some probing questions." She tilted her head slightly, as if she was evaluating how to approach a task.

"Ask away," Diane quipped. "I'll try to give you the most honest and grandmotherly answer I can."

"How long ago did you get divorced?" Tamsin asked the question Diane was expecting.

"Five years ago." Diane looked down at her hands that were fidgeting with the edge of her blouse. "It's kind of ridiculous how stereotypical the whole thing was. Middle-aged man falls in love with hot young thing at the office. They have an affair behind his wife's back for a while, until the young mistress gives the man an ultimatum: leave the wife or be cut off from the constant supply of exciting and adventurous sex she provides. Not a very hard choice to make for a man in the throes of a mid-life crisis." Diane looked up again into Tamsin's kind face. "Those were not Lawrence's exact words, but that's what I understood from them."

Tamsin looked at her sympathetically. "I'm very sorry you had to go through that. Having to see him with Debbie at the club must be so hard, as well. Did you not feel like leaving, finding a new place to play?"

"I thought about it for a while," Diane said softly. "I even stayed away for a couple of months. But then I realised leaving the club would be admitting defeat in some way. I had already lost my husband and the life I knew and loved. I was not going to lose my circle of friends as well. So I stayed."

"I think you were very brave to do that." Tamsin held up her glass again. "To being brave," she said.

"Admittedly, Isabelle had a big part in helping me reach that decision. She was an invaluable source of support through the whole ordeal. So I'll drink to her." Diane held up her glass as well.

"To Isabelle then." Tamsin took a sip from her wine. "Can I ask another question?"

"Of course," Diane gazed at Tamsin. She didn't seem to be affected by the generous amount of wine they had already consumed. Diane, on the other hand, could not deny the pleasant tipsiness she felt.

"Have you been with anyone since the divorce? Gone on any dates?"

Diane smiled. The question was not unexpected considering the topic of conversation. "I haven't," she said. "Timothy and I talked about this just the other day. He said I should go on a cruise or some kind of group trip for mature singles." Diane scoffed. "He even suggested I sign up for a dating site. Can you imagine: me, a soon-to-be granny, on Timber, or whatever it's called?"

Tamsin let out a yelp. "Do you mean Tinder? There are loads of eligible bachelors your age on there."

"Oh, I don't doubt that," Diane said, "but they're all looking for women half their age." She squinted at Tamsin. "Are you on Tinder? Is that how you know who's on there?"

Tamsin seemed a little flustered at Diane's question. "Er, yes, I do have a Tinder profile. Not that I would have encountered any middle-aged men on there, since I only checked the box for women when I signed up."

Diane pondered this. She had so many questions for Tamsin. She decided to start at the beginning. "Have you always known you were attracted to women?"

"For as long as I can remember. As soon as my girlfriends at school started talking about boys and kissing them, I knew boys weren't for me. I only wanted to kiss my friend Nicole, so that was that."

"I kissed a girl once," Diane blurted out. *Damn that wine.*

Tamsin brought her hand to her mouth in shock, but Diane

could see the amusement in her eyes. "You did? Tell me all about it."

"That too was a perfect cliché." Diane chuckled. "I was at an all-girls boarding school. We were sixteen and wanted to practice for when we'd meet the boys from the neighbouring all-boys school at the yearly dance."

Diane fell silent as her mind travelled back to that afternoon, sitting on her bed with her roommate Fiona. They had practiced on their forearms first, before bringing their mouths together for a chaste kiss. After a few of those Fiona had suggested they open their mouths. Diane remembered the sensation of butterflies being released in her tummy as Fiona's tongue had tentatively made contact with hers. It was like nothing she'd ever felt before.

A cough brought her out of her reverie before the memory of the kiss could make way for the memory of what had happened after it. Tamsin was watching her with an amused expression on her face. "I'm guessing it was not an unpleasant experience, judging by the smile on your lips just now."

Diane's cheeks started to burn. "It was such a long time ago; I can hardly remember." She should stop drinking now. The wine was clearly causing her brain to play tricks on her. As she was replaying that adolescent kiss in her mind, the image of Fiona had blurred and gradually morphed into someone else. *Tamsin.* And the butterflies she'd remembered were now fluttering about inside her as she sat across from Tamsin.

Tamsin stayed quiet, but her expression showed she knew there was something going on.

"I think I've had a bit too much to drink," Diane said, putting her glass down on the table. If she wanted to make a somewhat elegant retreat before she embarrassed herself any more, now was the time to do so. "Thank you for the wine." She stood and gave Tamsin a small smile. "Good night."

"Good night, Diane," Tamsin said, a puzzled look on her face.

As Diane hurried to her room, she tried to reassure herself that it was just the wine that had caused Tamsin to appear in her memory of the kiss. But somehow she couldn't shake the feeling that the wine had only played a small part.

CHAPTER TEN

As soon as she opened her eyes, Tamsin brought her hands to her head. That Portuguese wine she'd indulged in the night before might have been delicious, but it was leaving some very painful reminders this morning. Her thoughts wandered to Diane. How was she feeling this morning? She'd soon find out at breakfast.

Spring was well on its way and rays of morning sun slanted in through the gap in the curtains. Tamsin forced herself out of bed and glanced outside the window. Her room overlooked the golf course and, at the sight of it, her heart filled with joy, erasing part of her hangover instantly.

What she'd told Diane last night about loving her job hadn't been an exaggeration. Tamsin had always wanted to be a teacher, but she'd never dreamed she could become a golf pro. Yet, here she was. Overlooking a beautiful Portuguese golf course on a gorgeous spring morning. This was her work —her life.

Her thoughts drifted back to Diane, who had been more than candid—and surprisingly understanding about Ellen. Tamsin looked forward to confiding in her again.

Even though Tamsin was a people person, it wasn't often that she met someone she so instantly clicked with. Someone with whom she could spend an evening drinking wine.

She had a private chuckle at Diane's confession about having kissed a classmate in boarding school. Tamsin herself had kissed many a girl during her school years. The main difference was that Tamsin had never stopped kissing girls.

She hopped into the shower and got ready for breakfast, and another full day of golf and sunshine.

———

Tamsin was just making a mess of removing the top from a soft-boiled egg when Isabelle turned up.

"Morning," she said, her voice overly cheerful.

"Good morning, Isabelle. Did you sleep well?" Tamsin nodded at the empty seat opposite her.

Isabelle pulled back the chair and sat down. Her bottom had barely touched the seat when a waiter turned up to ask if she wanted coffee or tea with her breakfast.

Isabelle ordered 'strong tea', then looked at Tamsin. "You know how it is the first night in a strange bed." She held her hand in front of her mouth as she suppressed a yawn. "And Diane's drunk snoring didn't help." She inclined her head. "How many bottles of that wine did you knock back?" Her lips curved into a smile.

"Just a few glasses." She smiled back at Isabelle. "Should I take her up some ibuprofen?"

"She'll be all right. Things are just going a bit slower for her this morning." Isabelle chuckled. "She'd kill me if she knew I was telling you this, by the way. As far as you know, Diane jumped out of bed this morning, fresh as a daisy."

"Just like I did," Tamsin said. "No wine for me tonight."

"May we join you?" Maggie and Barbara had materialised next to their table.

"Of course," Tamsin said. The waiter came by again and Tamsin focused some more on beheading her egg.

The ladies chattered among themselves, trying to engage Tamsin in their conversations as much as possible. As Tamsin dipped a crust of bread into the soft egg yolk, she believed her future at the RTGB looked far rosier than it had done at her previous club.

————

The ladies were playing a complete 18-hole round that morning. Tamsin had waited for Diane to turn up, but she'd missed the last possible tee time Tamsin could give her.

She asked Isabelle which room they were in and decided to check up on her.

Tamsin knocked on the door gently, but no response came. She knocked a second time with a bit more force.

"Diane. It's Tamsin," she said, hoping Diane could hear her.

There was some shuffling on the other side of the door, then a bang, followed by a muffled, "Damn it."

The door opened a crack, Diane's face appearing in it.

"Morning," Tamsin said. "Are you not joining us?"

"Good god, Tamsin." Diane briefly blinked her eyes shut. "I thought I was fine." She opened the door a little wider. "I was all dressed and ready to go, but then I got this dizzy spell. I decided to have a bit more of a lie-down."

"A dizzy spell?" Tamsin scrutinised Diane's face. Her eyes were small, their gaze unfocused. "Do you need a doctor?"

"For a hangover?" Diane managed a lighter version of her loud cackle of a laugh. "I don't think so." She opened the door all the way. "I was just about to order some room service. Do you want to come in for a coffee on the balcony?"

Tamsin looked at her watch. The others were on the course and it would be at least two hours before the first ones finished. "Why not?"

After Diane placed the call to room service, she joined Tamsin on the balcony.

"If you crane your neck like this, you can see some of the ladies on the green of the seventh," Tamsin said. "That makes me feel less guilty for sitting here on my backside with you."

"You're sort of watching them," Diane said, with a snicker. "What more can be expected of you?"

"Maggie has booked me for a lesson this afternoon," Tamsin said.

"You're looking after me now," Diane said.

"All in a day's work." Tamsin glanced at her. The light caught in her blonde highlights. Under the glaring light of the sun, Diane looked a little worse for wear. "How are you feeling?" she asked.

"Better, and after a good pot of coffee I might feel completely like myself again." Just then, the bell rang.

"Why don't I get that?" Tamsin rose and took possession of the tray which carried a large French press and two cups.

She brought them out onto the balcony and poured them each a cup.

"Thank you." Diane locked her gaze with hers for a split second—her eyes were a peculiar kind of light blue-grey—and smiled. "Also for checking on me."

"Well, if you look at it the other way, I'm partly responsible for your hungover state this morning, so it's the least I can do."

"You bought the first drink." Diane sipped from her coffee and her face visibly relaxed. "But that doesn't make you responsible, although I'd be more than glad to shift the blame on you."

"It was the first evening of your holiday and you'd won a very important competition. There's no blame to be cast here."

Tamsin smiled as she drank from her coffee. She wasn't a connoisseur by a long shot, but she recognised a good cup of coffee when she came across it. This one was certainly doing the trick.

"I had a good time, though." Diane painted on a grin. "You're so much more fun than Darren."

"Did Darren join the Ladies' trip?" Tamsin asked.

"Goodness no." There was mock-outrage in Diane's voice. "The poor man would have been clobbered to death with attention from the widows and divorcees." She chuckled. "All joking aside, the club is quite traditional like that. I don't suppose you've been asked to join the Gentlemen's trip to the South of France next month?"

"I suggested going along, but the club secretary advised against it."

Diane shook her head. "It's so silly, I mean, what with you, um, being a lesbian."

Tamsin burst out laughing. "Indeed it is. But don't worry, I haven't had any indecent proposals yet."

"This trip has only just started. Wait until the last evening. I suspect that's when a few of the ladies will make their move."

Tamsin joined Diane in her raucous laughter. "This is probably very indiscreet and do tell me if I'm out of bounds, but are any of the ladies on this trip *not* heterosexual?" Tamsin didn't quite know why she used the phrasing 'not heterosexual' while she could have just asked if any of them were lesbian or bisexual. It was something about the vibe in traditional golf clubs that made even Tamsin—who'd been out and proud for a good many years—use flowery language.

Diane's eyes grew wide. She obviously hadn't expected the question. Were her cheeks growing pink? "Not as far as I know." She regrouped. "There must be a few lesbians amongst the younger members, I'm sure, but not amongst this lot. That I know of, at least." A sparkle shone in her eyes. "Well, there have been rumours about Barbara because that's just what happens when a woman never marries and is never seen with a male companion."

Tamsin pictured Barbara. Next time she spoke to her, she'd try to scout for a vibe—a ping on her gaydar.

All of a sudden they heard a clattering in the trees between the course and the hotel grounds, and saw a ball land on the grass, a few yards away from the hotel.

"Goodness me," Diane said. "What's that ball doing there?"

"The dangers of having a room with a view over the course," Tamsin said. "Someone must have seriously mishit."

A couple of minutes later Maggie emerged from the trees, in search of the wayward ball.

"Maggie," Diane shouted, "it's closer to the building."

"Hello, ladies of leisure," Maggie said, waving at them. "Life's all right for some."

"How's it going?" Diane asked.

"This course is so beautiful, Diane," Maggie said. Barbara had just caught up with her.

Tamsin looked at her with different eyes. Of course, in a golf outfit, anyone could look like a lesbian. She'd long ago learned it wasn't about clothes or hairstyles or anything you could spot on the outside. She made a mental note to keep an eye on Barbara for the rest of this trip, and resist making any further assumptions.

"Diane, you lazy arse," Barbara said. "I can't believe you're sitting there drinking coffee. This is a golf trip, for heaven's sake, not a sit on your backside and drink coffee trip. Come down and enjoy the sunshine."

"She's right," Tamsin said. "How about we go to the practice grounds and work on your bunker shots while we wait for the others to finish?"

CHAPTER ELEVEN

O n the last night of the trip all the ladies were having dinner together on the hotel terrace. Large platters of seafood were placed in the middle of the two tables they occupied.

"Ouch," Isabelle exclaimed. "I think this langoustine is still alive, it's fighting so hard against being peeled."

Diane laughed. "You're just afraid of damaging your manicure." That morning Isabelle had declared she'd had enough of playing golf, after three days of it, and she'd gone off for a day of pampering at the hotel spa.

"Of course I am," Isabelle said. "Aren't my nails pretty?" She held out her hands in front of Diane again.

"Yes, yes, dear." Diane patted her arm. "For the fifth time, your nails look exquisite."

The sound of a piece of cutlery being tapped against a glass interrupted their banter.

"Ladies," Suzanna's voice boomed from the other table. "As this is our last evening before we fly back to the UK, I have prepared a few words."

"Here we go," Isabelle muttered. "Let's hope she keeps it

briefer than her speech at last year's season closing dinner."

"Shush," Diane scolded her. "Be nice."

"I want to thank you all for coming on this fabulous trip," Suzanna was saying. "I think we can all agree it was great to get away from the British weather and enjoy this wonderful sunshine…"

Isabelle nudged Diane. "Any second now, she's going to thank Tamsin for improving her game."

"I would like to give a special thank-you to Tamsin for helping us all improve our game."

Diane snorted a laugh and took a mouthful of wine to cover it. Everyone else applauded in agreement.

"It was great to get to know our new pro in this beautiful setting. And now I think Tamsin would like to say a few words." Suzanna turned towards Tamsin, who was sitting next to her.

Tamsin stood and towered over Suzanna by at least a head. She cleared her throat with a little cough. "First of all, I want to thank Suzanna for the great organisation and for taking such good care of all the logistics." She paused as the ladies gave a polite applause.

Tamsin seemed at ease speaking in front of an audience. Diane could only admire this, as she herself was petrified just at the thought of it. She had declined the role of Lady Captain several times over the years, scared by the thought of having to give a speech after every Ladies' Day competition.

"Most of all," Tamsin continued, "I want to thank all of you ladies for being so friendly and welcoming to me. A few of you I met here for the first time, and some of you I had the pleasure of knowing already." Tamsin looked straight at Diane as she said this. "It has been wonderful to spend this time with you, both on the golf course and off. I feel like I have made new friends, which will make settling into my new home so much easier."

Diane's eyes were locked on Tamsin's as if they were tethered to each other.

The rest of the room faded away and Tamsin was speaking only to her. After a while Tamsin's words barely even registered anymore as Diane sat staring at her. A feeling of want started in her gut and swelled with every second that passed.

"I could not have hoped for a better introduction to the RTGC and I hope to see you all often on the course." Tamsin's gaze went around the assembled ladies now and Diane's awareness was brought back to the room. "And you know where to reach me to book a lesson."

Everyone laughed and clapped their hands vigorously.

Tamsin sat down and Diane saw Suzanna pat her on the back, offering her own congratulations. She felt a pang of regret at not having been sat at the same table as Tamsin.

"What's the matter with you?" Isabelle said. "You look like someone just ran over your bunny."

"Sorry," Diane answered, "I was lost in thought. And I don't have a bunny." She slapped Isabelle playfully on the shoulder. She smiled at her friend, but couldn't shake the troubling thought that had dawned on her: could it be that the regret at not sitting next to Tamsin on this last evening was actually jealousy?

———

Diane tapped the 'Check In' button on the screen of her tablet. The flight back to London was at nine the next morning, and she wanted to just drop off her bags at the counter and head to the departure lounge. No waiting in line to check in for her.

She went through her carry-on bag to make sure she had everything she needed for the journey home. Her passport and purse were there, but she couldn't find the book she was reading. She looked over to her bedside table, but the book wasn't there either.

Diane had taken it down to dinner to show Judy. She could have sworn she had brought it back up again after the meal, but maybe she'd left it downstairs.

She knocked on the bathroom door and said, "I'm going down to the restaurant, I think I forgot my book."

Isabelle came out of the bathroom. "I'll probably be asleep by the time you get back, I'm exhausted." She gave Diane a kiss on the cheek. "Sleep well."

Diane took the stairs and went straight to the terrace, where her book was still lying on the table she'd been sitting at. As she walked through the lobby, she spotted Tamsin at a table in the hotel bar with a glass of wine in front of her.

Diane hesitated. She wanted to get enough sleep before her alarm went off at six tomorrow, but her feet seemed to be of a different mind and started to walk towards Tamsin.

"Having a night cap?" Diane found herself asking.

Tamsin looked up to Diane with a smile on her face. "I am indeed. Will you join me?" She didn't seem at all surprised that Diane had showed up.

"I don't want to disturb you if you're enjoying a bit of time alone, after four days with a bunch of cackling women." Diane made to walk away.

Tamsin waved off her comment. "Please, sit," she insisted. "To be honest, I was kind of hoping you'd come back down again. I really enjoyed our bender on the first night. It's only fitting we do it again on the last one."

Tamsin's smile reignited the want that had manifested itself in Diane earlier. She sat opposite Tamsin and gestured to the waiter to bring them two glasses of wine.

"I can't argue with that," Diane said, smiling back at Tamsin. "Although I could do without a hangover since we're going to be stuck on a plane for three hours."

64

"Then we'll just have the one," Tamsin said, as the waiter deposited their drinks on the table. She picked up her glass and held it up.

Diane did the same. "What should we drink to this time?"

Tamsin seemed to give this some thought, all the while keeping her green eyes trained on Diane. "To new beginnings," she said simply.

Diane clinked her glass against Tamsin's and took a sip. She assumed Tamsin was talking about her own new beginning at the RTGC, but she couldn't help but feel there was something more to the toast.

"Did you have a nice time?" Diane usually wasn't one for small-talk, but she found herself at a loss for more meaningful words.

Tamsin was still looking at her intently. "I had a lovely time. You ladies are a pretty nice bunch. I would be happy to go on another group trip with most of you." Her smile turned cheeky at this comment.

"Most of us?" Diane was puzzled. "Who would you not want to go with?"

"What I meant was, there are a few of you—one of you especially—whom I wouldn't mind going on a solo trip with." Tamsin's smile disappeared for a brief moment and her face turned anxious, as if she'd just realised that she'd said something inappropriate. "For more intensive coaching, I mean. It's difficult to give everyone enough of my time and attention on these group outings."

"Of course," Diane said, regarding Tamsin. *Did she just say what I think she said?* Surely she wasn't really talking about golf lessons?

Diane couldn't be sure which "one" Tamsin was referring to. To her knowledge, she was the person with whom Tamsin had spent the most time outside of the group activities. A glow warmed her. She took a sip of wine to hide her flushed cheeks, but she didn't want to drink too fast. She found herself wanting to make their one drink together last as long as she possibly could.

Why was that? Was Tamsin flirting? Did Diane want to flirt back? And if she did, what did it mean? It had been a long time since anyone had shown any romantic interest in her. She had loved Lawrence dearly, but even she had to admit that in the last few years of their marriage they had been more like friends than passionate lovers.

But the thing was, she *did* feel like flirting back at Tamsin. If indeed, that was what was happening.

"I, er," Diane started, unsure of how to proceed. Then the words seemed to come to her of their own accord. "I wasn't entirely honest with you the other night. When I said I had never had any romantic feelings for a woman." She paused, trying to assess what Tamsin was thinking of this seemingly abrupt change of topic.

Tamsin's lips formed into a smile again and she looked at Diane expectantly. "You weren't?" Her voice was gentle.

"No," Diane continued, encouraged by the look on Tamsin's face. "After we talked the other night, I thought back some more to my time at boarding school. I realised that the girl I mentioned, the one I 'practiced' with"—she made air quotes with her fingers—"well, I was probably a little in love with her. After the kissing incident, she started spending a lot of time with another one of our classmates, and I felt completely cast aside. Until now, I always thought it was just the disappointment of losing a friend. But I really felt terrible for a long time, and I missed her so much. Looking back, I realise that what I was actually feeling was rejection and jealousy."

Diane's gaze had drifted to Tamsin's mouth while she was talking and it was almost like she was hypnotised by Tamsin's lips, by her smile.

"Interesting," Tamsin said.

The words snapped Diane out of her trance-like state and she looked up at Tamsin's eyes. Where before they had looked at her with only kindness, they now exuded something else. What it was, Diane wasn't sure, but it caused a flurry of heat to spread throughout her body.

Diane couldn't remember the last time she'd felt like this. Probably never. The unfamiliarity of it just increased her confusion. She knew it was her turn to say something, that she should probably expand on what she'd just revealed.

But no words came to her, so she said the only thing she could. "I should go up to my room." She rose from her chair.

Tamsin stood as well. "Diane, wait."

"Isabelle will be wondering where I am." Diane started walking away. "I'll see you tomorrow morning," she said over her shoulder and almost ran to the stairs.

By the time she got to the first floor her mind was a whirlpool of questions and confusion. She was right back at boarding school, a bumbling teenage girl, overwhelmed by emotions she was not equipped to handle.

She reached her room but didn't go in immediately. Instead, she leaned her back against the wall and closed her eyes, inhaling and exhaling deeply to try and steady herself. She had to regain her composure before entering the room, in case Isabelle was still awake. Her friend would know instantly that something was not right.

After a few deep breaths her mind seemed to settle somewhat; the questions that had been swirling around retreated to the background and the logical side of her brain took over again. What had she been thinking, trying to flirt with a much younger woman? It had just been a flash of temporary insanity, a silly whim brought on by too much wine. Diane kept repeating this over and over as she opened the door to the room. But even to herself she didn't sound completely convincing.

CHAPTER TWELVE

T amsin leaned back against the headrest of her plane seat. She hadn't slept well and hoped to catch up on some much-needed rest, although her prospects for doing so didn't look promising. The chattering of middle-aged ladies, some of them with a nice tan on their faces, wasn't conducive to a power nap.

She'd asked for the window seat so she could at least stare outside—if she looked to her right, she would see Diane sitting at the other end of the three-seat row.

Diane.

All through the night, Tamsin had asked herself the same question: why had she said that silly thing about the solo trip? It had flummoxed them both to the extent that Diane had barely finished her glass of wine.

For the life of her, Tamsin couldn't figure out why those words had left her mouth. She liked Diane, there was no denying that. But not like *that*. Diane was as far removed from the type of women Tamsin usually fell for as could be. Moreover, she was a prominent member of her new club. And a heterosexual divorced accountant. Sure, she could be in that phase of her life where she might be questioning certain aspects of it—like so many women before her, and the many that would follow—but Tamsin wasn't one to exploit that kind of vulnerability.

She might fall for what most of her friends and family dubbed 'the wrong kind of woman for her' at regular intervals, but at least Tamsin didn't have a penchant for falling for supposedly straight women. Even though her father certainly wished she were, Ellen had decidedly not been straight.

Of all the thoughts floating through her mind after a successful first trip away with the RTGC ladies, a tipsy—because surely she must have been?—flirt with Diane Thompson was the last thing she'd expected. But what had been more unsettling, was that Diane had flirted back. There was an energy between them, a magnetism that drew them to each other, made them seek out each other's company in a group—although Diane sitting in the same row as her was a coincidence.

Tamsin gazed out of the window. They'd left the white beaches and blue waters of Portugal behind and were cruising above a carpet of clouds, which meant that Tamsin couldn't see much of anything. But it was better than looking to her right and seeing Diane.

She couldn't afford to screw up another job because of something like this. What had happened with Ellen was bad enough, but still easy enough to recover from. If something like that happened again, however, she'd be stuck with a reputation she'd never be able to get rid of—and she could kiss her golf pro career goodbye.

Tamsin closed her eyes. Sleep wouldn't come, but she would use all the mental energy she had left to squash any thoughts of her and Diane. There was no such thing. She wasn't even attracted to her.

Tamsin would have given anything to get off the plane right

there and then. She needed a few days on her own to sort out her thoughts—and herself. Long walks through the forest near her cottage with Bramble. A few hours spent restoring that old desk she'd bought a few months ago but hadn't done anything with yet. Maybe another Tinder date… with someone who was her type. Yes, that was what she needed. She started planning the next few days in her head in great detail, just to have something to hold on to while her mind was in turmoil. Bramble. Forest. Desk. Tinder. She repeated the words in her head like a mantra so she didn't have to give in to the urge to look to her right—and catch a glimpse of Diane.

———

Some of the ladies' husbands had volunteered to pick them up at Gatwick airport, squeezing the single women—and their bulky golf bags—into their cars. In Barbara's case, her sister Camilla was fetching her and offered Tamsin a ride.

Goodbyes were said and Tamsin found herself being drawn into hug after hug, some stiff and forced, others generous and warm, until the only person she hadn't said goodbye to was Diane.

"Are you all right?" Diane asked. "You don't quite seem your jolly self today." She spoke as though the previous night hadn't happened.

"Just the end-of-trip blues," Tamsin said. "Back to reality and all that."

"It was rather a nice getaway, wasn't it?" Diane winked at her.

Tamsin was at a loss for words but, nevertheless, thought she should say something. She wasn't the kind to let sleeping dogs lie, and have this unease fester inside of her. She wanted to leave it here, at the airport, so she could move on. And set up another Tinder date.

"Can I talk to you for a minute?" Tamsin took a few steps backwards, although privacy in an airport arrivals hall would always be too much to ask for.

Diane followed her. "Something wrong?" she asked.

"About last night," Tamsin said. "It's important to me that you know I wasn't trying anything. I wouldn't. I mean, it wouldn't be right." Tamsin cursed herself for her lack of eloquence.

Diane emitted her loud squawk of a laugh. "Well, you can stop worrying then. The thought hadn't even crossed my mind." She patted Tamsin on the upper arm, quite a condescending gesture—or was it defensive?

"Good." Tamsin tried a smile, although she was pretty sure it didn't much look like one.

"You gave all the others one." Diane threw her arms wide. "My turn now for a hug."

Tamsin stepped into her embrace, uneasiness and something else—something she couldn't quite put a finger on—bubbling inside her.

Diane's hug was by far the warmest she'd received today, and she drew her in much tighter than any of the other ladies had.

"Call me to set up that appointment," Diane said, after they broke from their hug. "To do your books."

"Will do." Tamsin watched her saunter off. As usual, Diane was stylishly dressed in pleated trousers and matching blazer. *Who even wears clothes like that on a plane?* But of course, the inane question only served to mask the continuing turmoil in her mind.

———

The first thing Tamsin did when she arrived home, was leave

again. She got into her car to pick up Bramble at the kennels where she had reluctantly left her chocolate Labrador.

Bramble was elated to see her and nearly bowled Tamsin over with enthusiasm. She'd take her for a good long walk and promised herself to not leave her dog for four consecutive days any time soon.

As she walked through the forest, rejoicing in Bramble's obvious delight, she thought about what Diane had said. "Call me to set up an appointment." Before Diane had added that it would be an appointment to go over Tamsin's books, Tamsin had, again, for a split second, believed Diane had meant something else. Maybe because, deep down, it was what she'd wanted to hear.

Bramble rushed towards her, a battered tennis ball in her mouth. She dropped it in front of Tamsin's feet, who promptly threw it in between the trees to her left. Bramble bounded off again, leaving Tamsin alone with her thoughts. Why did Diane always appear to be a part of those?

They'd shared a few glasses of wine, a few laughs—Diane had such an infectious, raucous rumble of a laugh—and a couple of locked glances. So what?

Yet, no matter how far she walked with Bramble, penetrating deeper into the forest, not caring how long her walk home would take after what had already been an exhausting day of travel, Tamsin kept hearing Diane's voice, kept being reminded of that cheeky twinkle in her eyes when she'd confided in Tamsin about her boarding school same-sex kissing dalliance.

After she'd taken a long, hot shower, and was lying with her feet up on the sofa, a glass of wine in reach, Tamsin grabbed her phone. She had to do something to quench this malaise, this uprising in her blood. She had to go on a date. Preferably a date with a happy ending, although Tamsin wasn't really the type for that. She and Ellen had been going out for more than a month before Tamsin had allowed anything further to happen. She liked to be sure of her feelings, and the other person's feelings as well. But tonight, she didn't care about feelings. Tamsin was a woman in her prime, in good shape, with healthy urges. She hadn't expected a trip with a dozen ladies in conservative golf outfits to trigger this need, but there she sat, finger poised over her phone screen, ready to open the app.

She tapped and went into the search settings first. At least she wasn't going to make the mistake again of looking for someone too young. She was just scrolling, anyway. Swiping left, until she felt compelled to swipe right. She adjusted the age selection to up to thirty-seven—wasn't that a good compromise?—and the location selection to a twenty mile radius around Tynebury. Frankly, she wasn't expecting anyone to come up. But, through the marvels of modern technology and humankind's hunger for connection, Tamsin was presented with a surprising number of women seeking women.

Now all that was left was finding someone who tickled her fancy. Her thumb was just beginning to cramp up from swiping left all the time, when she came across the face of an agreeable-looking woman. She had short brown hair, a warm gaze in her brown eyes, and a pleasant smile on her lips. Tamsin liked the look of her—and that was really what it was all about with a shallow app like this. Before she could change her mind, she swiped right and hoped for the best: a return right swipe.

Now all she could do was wait.

She glanced at Bramble, who was lying on the rug as though she'd promptly fallen over, and reached for her glass of wine. She'd barely taken a sip when her phone chimed with a notification.

She picked it up again and saw it was from Tinder. Things were looking up.

CHAPTER THIRTEEN

Diane locked her car. She had managed to squeeze into the last available spot in the small carpark next to the Hare & Tortoise.

Even though she only worked part time, the last two days since she'd got back from Portugal had been quite hectic. The fiscal year was ending and it was the busiest period of the year at Thompson & Associates. It seemed like all her clients had decided while she was away that they wanted some aspect of their accounts re-evaluated in view of the Brexit fallout, and that this needed to happen straight away.

After two days of near constant meetings, Diane had decided to reward herself with a meal in her favourite gastropub in the next village.

"Good evening, Mrs Thompson," the maître d' greeted her. "I've saved your favourite table for you."

He led her to a small table in the front corner of the room, next to a window that overlooked the pub entrance.

"Thank you, David," she said, as he handed her a menu. "I'll have a gin and tonic right away, please. It's been quite a day."

"Of course," David said.

Diane checked the blackboard on which the daily specials were listed and decided on the crispy sweetbreads.

David promptly reappeared with her drink. Diane ordered her food and took a sip from the tall glass.

"Ah." She couldn't help herself from sighing in contentment at the fresh taste in her mouth.

Diane looked around the room. A few tables were occupied, but it was still quite early. The place would fill up soon enough.

In the first couple of years after the divorce, Diane had not gone out to eat very often. She had of course been out with friends and with Timothy and Lucy, but it had taken a long time for her to get used to dining out on her own. These days, she quite enjoyed the tranquillity of it. She usually read a book or just observed the people around her.

A movement outside caught the corner of her eye. Probably some diners arriving. The door to the restaurant opened and a young brown-haired woman walked in, followed by a familiar-looking figure.

Tamsin.

Diane had been so busy that she'd not really had time to think much about the pro, but seeing her now brought everything that had happened in Portugal back to the forefront of her mind.

When they had said goodbye at the airport, Diane had brushed off what had happened the night before as insignificant, at least in front of Tamsin. She thought she'd done quite a convincing job of acting nonchalant, while inside, she had felt the exact opposite.

She watched as David led Tamsin and her companion to a table in an alcove on the other side of the dining room. When they'd sat down, Diane had a partial view of Tamsin's back, but she was facing the other woman, albeit from a safe distance. Tamsin had not yet seen Diane, or if she had, she was doing a good job at pretending she hadn't.

Diane wondered who the woman was. Tamsin had mentioned a sister in London, but this woman looked nothing like Tamsin. She was much shorter than Tamsin and had a broad face with wide features, whereas Tamsin's face was longer and sharper.

A date, then? The two women did not look as comfortable in each other's presence as two people would who'd known each other a while. Maybe it was a first date. Not that Diane could remember how that felt.

A little knot tied itself in Diane's stomach at the thought that Tamsin might be on a date. It was a feeling she had never experienced before, at least that she could remember. Tamsin seemed to bring up a lot of unfamiliar feelings in Diane.

The first time she had seen Lawrence with Debbie on his arm, it had caused turmoil inside her, of course. She'd been uncomfortable, sad, and angry most of all. But she hadn't been jealous. She had not wanted to be in Debbie's place, whereas now, all she could think was that she wished she was the one sitting across from Tamsin.

The waiter arrived with her food and placed it in front of Diane. Her appetite seemed to have vanished, but she started taking a few small bites. The dish was delicious, but she couldn't even bring herself to eat half of it.

Diane took her book out from her bag and tried to focus on that instead of what was happening across the room, but she found her gaze wandering up and towards Tamsin's table every few minutes.

Tamsin's companion was looking around the restaurant, seemingly not paying that much attention to what Tamsin was saying. Diane couldn't imagine not hanging on every one of Tamsin's words if she were the one sitting across from her.

The woman's gaze finally landed on Diane and Diane looked down quickly at her book. She did her best to keep reading, but again her eyes seemed to have a mind of their own. When she glanced up next, she found Tamsin's date staring straight at her. The woman leaned over towards Tamsin and said something, which caused Tamsin to turn around and lock eyes with Diane.

Diane gave her a small wave and smile, trying hard to come across as normal as possible. Tamsin returned the wave and then turned back to her companion.

What was Tamsin saying to her date about the lady who kept staring at them from the other side of the dining room? *She's a lady from the club I work at. Divorced a few years ago, but still alone. A bit sad really, she seems to have a bit of a crush on me.*

Diane gave her head a small shake. What had brought on that thought? Surely, she didn't have a crush on a woman, let alone one fifteen years her junior.

To distract her mind from its current train of thought, she attempted to eat more of the sweetbreads but gave up after a few bites. She pushed the plate away.

As if by magic David appeared at her table. "Can I take this away, Mrs Thompson?"

"Yes, please," Diane said. "Tell the chef it was delicious, but I was not as hungry as I thought."

———

Diane washed her hands in the restaurant bathroom. She had quickly paid her bill after her plate had been taken away, skipping dessert or coffee, wanting to just head home.

The door to the bathroom opened. In the reflection of the mirror Diane saw Tamsin walk in and stop behind her.

"Diane," she said.

When nothing else seemed to be forthcoming, Diane turned around to face Tamsin, her hands dripping water onto the floor.

"Tamsin, how nice to see you," Diane said. "I see you've

discovered one of the area's hidden gastronomic secrets. This is the best place for a relaxed bite." Stop babbling, she told herself.

"Yes," Tamsin replied, "it's very nice. I, er…" She looked down at her feet. "Sarah chose it."

"Ah," Diane said. "Sarah has excellent taste, then. Is she…" Diane didn't know what she wanted to ask exactly.

"We're on a date. We met on Tinder." Tamsin gave a small chuckle.

"I see." Diane looked around for the hand dryer to give herself something to do while she figured out what to say next. She inserted her hands into the machine and the noise of the blower drowned out all possibility for a conversation. When her hands were dry she turned around to find Tamsin standing in the exact same spot.

"How's the date going?" Diane asked.

"Let's just say I doubt there'll be a second one." Tamsin smiled wryly.

"How come?" Diane asked with an unintended edge to her voice. "Is she too mature for your taste? I thought you liked them younger. At least that's what you told me." Diane couldn't believe what had come out of her own mouth.

The look of consternation on Tamsin's face told Diane that she had definitely overstepped some kind of boundary.

"I'm sorry," she said quickly. "That came out all wrong."

"Never mind." Tamsin disappeared into one of the stalls.

Diane heard the lock being secured forcefully. She stared at the door a few seconds longer before walking out of the bathroom and heading for the car park. She'd probably just ruined the first significant new friendship she'd made in years.

CHAPTER FOURTEEN

As soon as Tamsin had clocked Diane at the pub, as far as she was concerned, her date with Sarah had been over. The woman was nice enough and, just like Tamsin, loved doing up old furniture—and she only lived about ten miles from her.

Many boxes had been ticked, and Tamsin had been willing to give the whole thing a chance, despite Sarah being quite a few years older than the women she was used to dating—or perhaps even because of that. Then Sarah had mentioned the lady staring at them from across the restaurant. Diane sat there, alone at a table, looking her usual elegant self, perfectly styled, holding her cutlery in just the right way, and Tamsin had been transported back to Portugal. After that, try as she might, she'd been unable to focus her attention on Sarah.

After saying a polite goodbye to Sarah, Tamsin let Bramble out of the house for a bit of a run in the garden, before sinking down into one of the patio chairs to consider her options.

First on the agenda would be admitting to herself that she was attracted to Diane. She'd felt it so clearly in the pub, maybe because of the contrast with her feelings for her date. Every time Tamsin had come up with a question to further the conversation with Sarah, she'd wished she could have asked Diane instead. Diane, who was sitting only a few tables away from her, whose gaze Tamsin could feel burning into the back of her head.

"I'm attracted to her," Tamsin whispered. Bramble didn't look up. Darkness was falling and she was too busy eyeing the bats flying overhead. Tamsin leaned back in her chair and inhaled a lungful of fresh air. She could do that here in Tynebury. The air was clean and the streets were quiet. Bramble was no longer confined to a mostly indoor life, only broken up by two walks a day. Tamsin could have a good life here as well. She liked the club, the people, the village.

She liked Diane.

She could try to deny it all she wanted, but all the signs were there. The flutter in her chest when she'd caught sight of her. The almost irrepressible desire to send her a text message right there and then. The images of her graceful face drifting in and out of Tamsin's mind willy-nilly. And then Diane had gone and said something so unexpected, so baffling, that Tamsin had been given no other choice but to hide in the toilet cubicle. But she didn't really know Diane. They'd shared a few glasses of wine in Portugal, but so what? Clearly, the woman had a bit of a mean streak.

Tamsin whistled for Bramble to come to her. It was getting chilly and she was sick of thinking about Diane. Tamsin could like her all she wanted—there was no way she was getting involved with someone like that. And until proven otherwise, the woman was heterosexual. Tamsin should focus on that. And she was fifty-four, for crying out loud. And a member of the golf club. At least Diane's father wasn't club president, but in this case, that was not an advantage. Tamsin had learned her lesson.

Bramble sped up to her at high speed then slid to a stop. She lay panting at Tamsin's feet, so that Tamsin could scratch her behind the ears. Diane probably wasn't a dog person, either. She looked far too polished for that.

"Come on then." Tamsin rose and Bramble followed her. "Time for bed."

As she walked into the cottage, she vowed to put Diane Thompson out of her head and, this time, she'd do it without the help of Tinder.

———

The next morning, Tamsin had planned to do some accounting, but as soon as she sat at her desk and cast a glance over the folder where she kept her receipts, her heart sank. Being a golf pro meant being a freelancer, which brought with it the only aspect of her job she truly despised: administration. Tamsin revelled in giving a pupil a crucial tip on how to hit the golf ball a few yards further, on how to get their putting more precise. She delighted in being out there for a round of golf on her own—just her against the course. Getting her accounts in order didn't have anything to do with that, yet it was a critical part of how she made a living.

Maxine, her accountant in Croydon, had sent her a bunch of spreadsheets and a summary of her accounts, so she could have a go at filing her quarterly VAT return herself, but Tamsin had only to look at the green colour of the Excel logo for her stomach to twist. Green was her favourite colour, yet this particular hue made her want to look away in disgust.

Tamsin had never been able to trace back her acute dislike of anything mathematical. Her sister was the same, even though their mother's job as a risk analyst at an insurance company had been awash with numbers and calculations and complicated arithmetic. She and Eve both took after their much more artistic father, who made furniture out of any piece of wood he could lay his hands on.

Tamsin glanced at the picture of her mother on the mantle next to her desk. She looked her radiant, buoyant self in it. She had died almost eight years ago but when Tamsin looked at that picture and stared into her mother's soulful brown eyes, to Tamsin, it felt like she'd only passed eight days ago. The grief could still hit her like that, mercilessly and with such impact, and Tamsin knew it would always be like that. As long as she lived, she would miss her mum.

If only she could call and ask for her mother's help with the accounts. Her mum would have been all over it. Tamsin could still so easily picture her, sitting at one end of the dining table, a bunch of papers spread out in front of her. Every Sunday evening, without fault, she filled in a notebook with the amounts they'd spent that week. She kept a budget so meticulously and with such zeal, Tamsin often wondered why none of that had rubbed off on her. But she and her sister had always hated maths and their mother had never been able to stop herself from helping them with their homework. Come to think of it, their mum was the reason she and Eve couldn't do a complicated calculation even if their life depended on it.

"Thanks, Mum," Tamsin said to her picture. They'd often teased her about it. Even when she'd been so sick, her body so weakened by the chemo, her brain shot to pieces, they'd still tell her stories of how when they were younger they'd been unable to calculate the correct change to get back when they were sent to the shop.

She toyed with the idea of just mailing the folder to Maxine and letting her sort it all out. Or she could drive up, make a quick visit to her sister and enjoy a bite to eat in London. But this quarter's deadline was looming, and Tamsin had been way too lax about it. To be honest, she'd skilfully buried her head in the sand every time she'd caught a glimpse of the folder, and had, once again, excelled at putting it out of her mind.

Why was it so easy to forget about this while other thoughts were so incredibly persistent? Because there it was again. *Diane*. The local accountant. Her business card burning a hole in Tamsin's purse. Hiring Diane as her accountant would not help towards getting the woman off her mind. So far, Tamsin had only seen her in a leisurely environment, but what would she look like in the office? The big boss of her own company. Tamsin had no trouble picturing Diane, head high, shoulders back, delegating tasks and reigning supreme over her accountancy empire. Tamsin had to chuckle at the thought.

She rose and walked to the window. A magpie flew low over the lawn. Bramble, who was lazing on a blanket near the window, lifted her head a fraction, only to promptly put it back down again.

When her phone started ringing, Tamsin was relieved to be pulled from her tailspin of thoughts. She hoped it would be someone wanting to book a lesson, even if it meant having to do more accounting.

She picked up her phone from the desk. Speak of the devil.

"Hi, Diane," she said, stopping the glee she was feeling from seeping into her voice.

"Tamsin." Diane sounded matter-of-fact.

"What can I do for you?" Glee was quickly making way for something else. But maybe this was the universe making a decision for her, Tamsin thought. She needed a new accountant and, just like that, she was on the phone with one. She just needed to ignore the fact that said accountant was Diane, whom, she had definitively concluded last night, she was hopelessly attracted to.

"I didn't feel quite right with how we left things last night. I was rude and I would like to apologise."

"It's fine," Tamsin said. "No need for that. Things get blurted out sometimes. I understand."

"No, no, no. It's far from fine. I would like to formally apologise, which is the purpose of this phone call."

Tamsin tried hard to suppress a smile from spreading on her face. It would be hopeless to try and consciously ignore this crush. She was hardly an expert when it came to behavioural psychology, but she knew that much. Everybody knew. Try not to think of someone and all you'll end up doing is obsessing over them. "Apology formally accepted," Tamsin said. "Actually, now that I've got you on the phone, Diane." She sighed. "I'm in very, *very* dire need of an accountant."

"Well then, you're very much in luck. I was hoping to add the new RTGC pro to my client list. I'll be in the office in one hour. Would you like to come by?"

"That would most likely save me quite a bit of bother from Her Majesty's Revenue and Customs."

"I'll be expecting you then." Diane's voice had changed from matter-of-fact to smooth and almost melodic.

"See you in an hour then." They hung up and Tamsin took a deep breath. So much for trying to get Diane Thompson out of her head.

CHAPTER FIFTEEN

"Tamsin Foxley is here for you," Diane's receptionist informed her on the phone.

"Show her to my office please, Stacey."

A minute later a knock sounded on the door. Stacey ushered Tamsin in and asked, "Can I bring you anything to drink?"

Diane sent Tamsin a questioning look. "Tea?"

"That would be great," Tamsin said.

Stacey hurried off, closing the door behind her.

Tamsin stood in the middle of Diane's office, holding two bulky binders in her arms. "I come bearing gifts," she said, a hint of sarcasm in her voice.

"Let me help you with those." Diane took hold of the binders and placed them on the conference table. She turned back towards Tamsin, who was still standing in the same spot.

Tamsin offered Diane a warm smile. "Thank you for seeing me at such short notice."

Diane waved her hand dismissively. "That's quite all right. Happy to help. Shall we sit?" She pointed at the conference table and took the chair at the head, pulling out the one to her left for Tamsin.

"This is quite the office you have here," Tamsin said. "I feel like I'm in the City rather than a small village in Sussex."

"I suppose," Diane replied. "It wasn't always like this. I started out on my own. But business took off over the years and I had to grow and hire people." Diane couldn't help a hint of pride from slipping into her words. "And now I think we're one of the largest accountancy firms this side of London."

"Colour me impressed," Tamsin said. "I appreciate even more the time you're giving me then." The look she gave Diane was grateful, but there was something else in there as well. An intensity that wasn't there before—or maybe Diane hadn't noticed it.

"So," Diane said, grabbing one of the binders, "what have you brought me?"

Tamsin showed Diane the documents she had amassed during the past year. They spent the next half hour going over them and preparing Tamsin's filing.

"It seems quite straightforward," Diane said when they'd finished. "You can leave these with me and we'll have a proposal for you soon."

"Thank you so much," Tamsin said. "You have no idea how much I hate all of this. I'll take a day on the driving range in pouring rain over even an hour of paperwork any time."

"It's what we're here for." Diane smiled at Tamsin, a wave of joy washing over her at Tamsin's obvious gratitude. She also felt a compelling need to please Tamsin, more than she'd ever experienced with any other client.

"What can I do to thank you?" Tamsin seemed to think for a moment. "How about I cook you dinner tonight? If you're not busy, of course."

Diane's heart did a little dance of joy at the invitation. "I'm free as a bird tonight, so I would love that."

"Splendid," Tamsin exclaimed. "If the weather stays like this we can even have a drink in the garden before. Say, around seven?"

"I'll be there," Diane said, already wanting the day to go by quickly so she could be in Tamsin's company again.

———

Diane pulled her car up in front of the little gate that sported an ornate sign for *Heather Cottage*. She had passed by many times before, but she'd never seen the inside of the small flint and brick cottage that was owned by the Andersons and now rented by Tamsin.

She opened the gate and stepped into the small front garden. She'd barely had time to close the gate before a chocolate Labrador bounded towards her from the side of the house. She held out her hand for the dog to sniff, before crouching down and giving it a rub behind the ears.

"Hello," Tamsin greeted her as she herself rounded the corner of the house. "I see you've met Bramble."

Diane stood back up. "She's gorgeous." She held out the bottle of red wine she had picked up at the shop on her way over. "Here you go. Thank you for inviting me."

Tamsin took the bottle and peered at the label. "Portuguese," she exclaimed. "How perfectly appropriate." She turned towards the cottage. "Come in. Let me give you a tour of my humble abode."

They walked into a small hallway and then through a door to the right. The room beyond was a sizeable open plan lounge, dining area and kitchen, with large French windows that looked out over the back garden. The furniture and appliances all looked brand new, but the house itself still had some period features: dark ceiling beams and an old fireplace set into the wall.

"Goodness," Diane said. "This is beautiful. I knew the Andersons had done some work on this place, but I had no idea it had turned out this lovely."

"Yes," Tamsin said, looking around the room as if she was still discovering it herself. "I can't believe how lucky I was that this place was available just when I was looking. It was exactly what I had in mind when I decided to move to the countryside."

Tamsin led Diane through the French windows and into the garden, where Bramble now sat on the patio chewing a huge bone.

"Please, sit while I get us some drinks. White wine all right with you to start off, or would you like something stronger? I think I have some gin."

"White wine would be great," Diane said. She sat in one of the two patio chairs that were set up on either side of a small teak table. The garden was showing the first signs of spring. She turned her face towards the low-hanging sun and closed her eyes, enjoying the subtle warmth on her skin.

She opened her eyes again at the sound of glasses being placed on the table. Tamsin hovered over it, the sun shielded behind her. It gave her a glowing orange halo, almost like an angel in a Renaissance painting. The vision sent a jolt of electricity through Diane that reached all the way to her core. Diane did not believe in the concept of the *coup de foudre*, but this... This almost felt like one. Dizziness overcame her and the blood seemed to drain from her face.

"Are you all right?" Tamsin asked, concern in her tone. "You look like you've just seen a ghost."

Diane tried to collect herself by holding her hand up to her face. "Just blinded by the sun in my eyes." She attempted to produce a convincing laugh. "I'm not used to it here in England."

Tamsin sat and handed Diane a glass. She held up her own

and said, "To the brave accountants who wade through piles of paperwork to make other people's lives easier."

"How very eloquently put," Diane said. She took a sip of the wine. "How was the rest of your day?"

"I taught a couple of classes. Not a full day's work yet, but that should change once Darren's gone. It did leave me with some time for a few holes by myself." Tamsin's face lit up. "Tynebury is such a lovely course. I still can't quite believe I'm lucky enough to spend so much time there."

"That it most definitely is. But we're the ones who are lucky that you decided to come and work there."

Tamsin giggled. "If you're hoping flattery will get you a free lesson, you're on the right track."

"I try my best," Diane said. Before she could say anything else, a loud bark came from beside her and Bramble shot off to the back of the garden to chase a bird.

"Bramble," Tamsin shouted, getting up and running after her. "Get back here."

She grabbed hold of the dog's collar and led her back towards the patio. "Sit," she ordered and Bramble meekly settled down again beside Diane's chair. "Sorry about that," Tamsin addressed Diane now. "There's a gap in the garden fence so I'm always scared she'll run off through it." She sat in her chair again. "Now, where were we? I think you were trying to flatter me into a free lesson." She sent Diane a mischievous grin.

"Give me some time and some more of this wine, and I'll come up with something." Diane felt her mouth pull into a grin to match Tamsin's.

Her gaze fixed on Tamsin's green eyes and they sat like that for a while, not saying a word. The silence stretched out between them. It wasn't uncomfortable, but with each passing second, Diane felt a sense of expectation grow. Expectation that was becoming too much for her to bear. Her glance skittered away from Tamsin.

"I hope you like fish," Tamsin said. "I have a beautiful piece of salmon lined up for us." Diane was grateful to her for moving the conversation to safer grounds.

"I love salmon," Diane said, bringing her gaze back to Tamsin. "And I can't wait to sample your culinary skills."

"I hope they'll meet your expectations." There was a flirty edge to Tamsin's tone. And to the smile she was giving Diane. Maybe this wasn't such an innocuous topic after all.

While this kind of back-and-forth felt unfamiliar to Diane, it was also exciting and adventurous.

"I'm sure you won't disappoint," Diane found herself saying, hoping to mirror Tamsin's flirty tone. Her gaze was still glued to Tamsin's, adding weight to the words she had just uttered.

A cloud moved in front of the sun, casting an almost instant chill on the patio. Diane felt a shiver go up her spine, but she wasn't sure if it was brought on by the change in temperature or the current vibe between her and Tamsin.

"Maybe we should move inside," Tamsin said. "It's starting to cool off. And I need to get to work in the kitchen."

————

They had moved from the garden to the dining table inside to eat.

"About the other night." Diane peered at Tamsin from behind her glass of wine.

Tamsin held her gaze.

"I didn't mean to cause offence. I was surprised to run into you and just blurted something out. I didn't mean a word of it."

Tamsin curled up the side of her mouth. "You did sound a bit harsh, but here we are." Her lips folded into a small smile. "You wouldn't be sitting here, eating this frankly delicious salmon, if I had taken offence." Tamsin straightened her shoulders. "I guess I was also a bit rattled because my date wasn't going very smoothly."

"Why was that, if I may ask?" A nervous flutter awoke in Diane's chest.

Tamsin pursed her lips. "It's hard to say exactly why sometimes. I guess we simply didn't hit it off. No chemistry, something like that."

Diane nodded. "The elusive chemistry." She tried a smile.

"What makes two people like each other?" Tamsin mused. "It's really hard to put your finger on, isn't it?"

Diane pondered this. She'd love to offer Tamsin some wise words, but she hadn't felt whatever it was that constituted 'chemistry' between two people in such a long time, she felt a little out of her depth. Unless... what she was feeling right now, and every time she was in Tamsin's vicinity for that matter, could be construed as such.

"It is." She looked into Tamsin's eyes. They sparkled with such intensity, that the flutter in Diane's chest flared up again. She had to look away. "I'm glad there are no hard feelings between us," she said. Only chemistry, she thought, but wouldn't dare say out loud.

———

"I should head home now," Diane said after she'd finished her coffee. "It's been a busy day and I have a nine o'clock tee time tomorrow morning." She stood and picked up her bag. "Dinner was lovely, thank you so much."

Tamsin stood as well and walked around the table. "I was happy to have you as my first official dinner guest."

Diane led the way to the front door. She turned to face her host. "Next time you'll have to come to mine. I don't have a

Bramble to provide entertainment but I'm a pretty good cook. At least that's what Timothy tells me."

"I would love that," Tamsin said.

Diane hesitated, not sure how to say goodbye. She took a step towards Tamsin and embraced her in a tentative hug, but once her arms were around her, they seemed to act on their own volition and squeezed her tighter. Tamsin responded to this by holding her closer still.

This embrace was stretching out much longer than was socially acceptable for two friends taking leave of each other, but Diane suddenly felt incapable of letting go. Until Tamsin's arms around her loosened slightly.

Diane pulled away. She couldn't look Tamsin in the eye. Something had definitely shifted inside her that evening and the woman she had just held so close to her was the cause of it.

"Well," Diane said, "I'm off then." She turned to the front door and pushed down the handle, but before she stepped out, she felt compelled to turn around again. Tamsin was staring at her with a strange look in her eyes.

Diane moved towards Tamsin and pecked her on the cheek. Then she turned and quickly walked towards the garden gate and her car without saying another word.

CHAPTER SIXTEEN

The next week, as Tamsin was going about her business, Diane kept popping into her head. She'd hardly seen her at the club, but Isabelle had told her that was normal at this time of year due to it being the end of the fiscal year. Which made Tamsin all the more grateful that Diane had taken her on as a new client, even though she was probably very busy. She hadn't let on during their meeting, and hadn't uttered a word about it during dinner.

Ah, that dinner. Not only had it been a sort of milestone for Tamsin to have her first guest over in her new house, but it had also been very pleasant to sit and chat with someone as evening fell. Tamsin hadn't always believed she was born for the kind of companionship that was touted everywhere, from movies to commercials to magazines, but maybe she had changed. And maybe Diane was part of her plan for that particular kind of change.

Maybe her move to the countryside had been about more than just wanting more space and fresh air. Perhaps the thought of turning forty soon had changed something in her subconscious and the results of that were only now making it to the surface.

She arrived home just as her sister's car was pulling up. She'd been looking forward to this weekend. And maybe she could confide in Eve. Tamsin felt she might burst if she didn't tell someone about Diane, even though there wasn't really that much to tell. It was just a feeling, in the end. Some chemicals in her brain acting up.

Eve got out of the car and opened her arms to pull Tamsin into a hug. "I'm so ready for a weekend without James," she said. She cast her glance over the cottage. "I'd forgotten how lovely and peaceful this place is. I've only just arrived and I feel a million times less stressed already."

Eve carried her holdall inside while Tamsin did the same with the shopping she'd picked up. When she was cooking for someone else but herself, she liked to put some effort in. On the menu tonight were scallops with courgette and black pudding.

Once inside, Bramble greeted Eve with a few licks of the hand. Tamsin opened the back door so Bramble could go out into the garden and chase squirrels. The sky was blanketed with thick dark clouds and Tamsin made a mental note to keep an eye out for rain. Bramble out in the rain equalled a big mess to clean up inside afterwards.

"Bramble seems to like it here." Eve produced two bottles of red wine from her bag. "James gave these to me and said to savour them. They're not meant for over-indulgence, apparently."

"As if we ever would."

"As if he won't be doing exactly that on his lads' weekend away." Eve rolled her eyes. "I can't believe I once argued for wanting to join him."

"Ah, the foolish things young love makes us do."

Eve set about opening the wine and pouring them each a glass while Tamsin started chopping a courgette.

"Can I help?"

Tamsin pointed to a chair by the kitchen door. "You can sit there and tell me all about your week."

"We spoke on the phone two days ago. Not much has happened since." Eve sat on the chair appointed to her. "I finished the drawings for the Clare Linderman book, so well done me." She sipped from her wine. "You tell me about your week instead."

"It was Darren's last week at the club." *Finally.* "So things should get a bit busier from now on."

"Which reminds me," Eve said. "I spoke to Maxine the other day when I was dropping off some documents. She asked if you'd managed to file your own taxes." She threw in a chuckle. "I told her that would be the day."

Something warm bloomed in Tamsin's chest. "I did no such foolish thing, of course. I've found an accountant here in the village. She's a member at the club. Her name's Diane." Tamsin focused on chopping, her head bent down. She didn't want a sudden blush on her cheeks while talking about Diane to give her away. This was Eve she was talking to, the foremost expert on all her feelings since the day she'd been born.

"*Aaaand?*"

"And what?" Tamsin still didn't look up.

"I recognise that certain inflection in your voice. Plus, it's not the first time you've mentioned this Diane."

"Don't be silly." Tamsin had a hard time focusing on cutting and, wishing to keep her fingers intact, she put the knife down for a moment. She even dared to look her sister in the eye. Eve's eyes were almost the same colour as hers, she thought, as she often did, even though she didn't know why. Despite being fraternal twins, they'd both inherited their mother's bright green eye colour, Eve's a little lighter than Tamsin's.

"I'm not the one being silly." Eve painted a smirk on her lips. "And I wasn't born yesterday either."

"Nope, you were born on the 6th of July 1978, just like me," Tamsin said, "albeit thirty minutes later than me, which technically makes me your older, much wiser sister." She smirked at Eve.

"Yeah, yeah, repeat that often enough and perhaps you'll believe it, but my thirty minutes deficit on this planet have not impacted my acquired wisdom at all." Eve put her glass of wine on the kitchen table. "How about you finish chopping first. You can tell me all about Diane later."

"There's nothing to—" Tamsin started, but Eve cut her off by lifting up her hand.

"At least, as my older sister, show me some respect."

They both burst out into a chuckle. 'Show some respect' was one of their father's mantras in life—and the man had many mantras to choose from.

"Have you seen Dad?" Tamsin inquired, glad that she was off the hook about telling her sister about Diane for now.

"No, but I'll see him next week. He's coming all the way to London. Some furniture vendor is very keen on a few of his latest pieces."

"Blimey, dad's leaving his territory and heading for the big smoke." Tamsin had resumed her chopping.

"You should come, Taz. It would be lovely to have a family dinner."

Tamsin nodded. "I will. What with the move and settling in here, I haven't seen dad in ages." When she still lived in London, Tamsin went to see her father at least once a month.

"It's a date then. We'll go to Lomax. He loves their rack of lamb."

Tamsin happily kept chopping, looking forward to seeing her father. When she took a break to sip her wine, her sister wagged a finger at her. "I'm going to set the table and, when we sit down, you and I are going to have a long overdue heart-to-heart."

———

Tamsin had managed to steer the conversation during dinner; a meal which didn't take very long because her sister always had the habit of gobbling her food as though she'd never be fed again in her life. Eve had started talking about an idea she'd had of transferring some of her drawings to the furniture their father made and she got so caught up in it, she seemed to have forgotten all about Diane.

If only it were that easy for Tamsin.

When they'd cleared their plates, Tamsin looked outside. Dusk was beginning to fall but no raindrops had yet made an appearance.

"Shall we take Bramble for her daily constitutional?" she asked.

"I thought you'd never ask. I want to see the nightlife in Tynebury." Eve smirked at her.

"I think Friday is karaoke night at the village pub," Tamsin replied.

"Let's steer clear of that then."

Tamsin grabbed Bramble's leash from a hook in the hallway. If they were walking into the village, she might need it.

Once outside, Eve inhaled deeply. "I can see the appeal, you know. Even though I've given you a hard time about moving to Dullsville."

"It's really not dull at all," Tamsin said. "It would be if you're looking for nightlife and a new restaurant opening every weekend, but I'm past that now."

Eve hooked an arm through Tamsin's. "You've settled in well, then?"

Tamsin nodded. "My job helps, of course. It's the perfect way to get to know people."

Eve squeezed her arm a little tighter. "True. It'd be different if you were a hermit." She tilted her head back and looked at the sky. "Weather's the same as in London, though."

"Are you glad we grew up in the countryside?" Tamsin asked.

"I guess." She shrugged. "Luckily, neither one of us have children of our own to take into account."

Eve had long ago declared her and James happily—and very consciously—child-free. Tamsin might have felt her biological clock give a little tick when she turned thirty, but she didn't think she had enough desire to consider becoming a single mother—and was further deterred by the whole rigmarole she'd have to go through. As far as Tamsin was concerned, children simply hadn't happened in her life. Most of the time, she was neither happy nor sad about that.

"I have Bramble, of course," Tamsin joked. The dog was walking a few feet ahead of them. "She loves growing up in the countryside."

Tamsin lived on the very edge of Tynebury, but the village wasn't big and it didn't take her and Eve long to reach the high street. The first few weeks after she had moved here, it had been downright bizarre to find everything but the pub closed on a Friday evening, so accustomed had Tamsin become to the convenience of living near a major city. But now it gave her a sense of peace. When there was nothing to be done, no new restaurants to try and no exciting plays to discover, it was much easier to relax—to simply do nothing.

"Where does Diane live?" Eve asked, out of the blue.

"I truly don't know. I've only been by her office, which is just off this street." Tamsin pointed at the next street on their left.

"Come on, Taz. Give me something. It's not as if I have my

own exciting love life to tell you about. James and I have been married for too long. We just muddle along and everything's fine."

"Everything can't be fine all the time," Tamsin said, buying time.

"Well, no, I guess not. So sometimes, for a little while, everything's not fine, until it's fine again." She bumped her hip into Tamsin's.

Then, as if the bump of her twin's hip opened up something inside of her, Tamsin started talking. The words were there, at the ready, as though they'd been waiting to be let out of her mouth. Tamsin told Eve about the evenings in Portugal, her resolution to get over Diane and subsequent failing to do so. About the dinner they'd had the previous week, ending with a hug that was very much open for interpretation.

She ended with, "but as far as I know, she's as straight as an arrow, so…"

"From what you're telling me, she doesn't sound very straight at all," Eve countered. "In fact, it sounds as though she's very much into you."

Tamsin stopped walking. She looked around but there was no one about. She'd have felt more comfortable conducting this conversation in the privacy of her home. "Sometimes, I get that impression as well."

"How old is she?" Eve let go of Tamsin's arm.

"Fifty-four," Tamsin said.

Eve's eyes widened. She put her hands on her hips. "Your tastes have certainly changed."

Tamsin wanted to object, but she barely had the chance to open her mouth before Eve interjected.

"Which just goes to show, a person's preferences can change all the time." She waggled her eyebrows. "What goes for you, can go for Diane too."

"Being interested in an older woman instead of a younger

one is a bit less drastic than going from men to women," Tamsin said.

"Sure," Eve said, "but that doesn't mean it doesn't happen." She offered her arm again. "Let's walk some more so you can listen to my sage advice."

Tamsin grabbed hold and they started walking through the quiet evening streets of Tynebury again.

"My advice," Eve said, "is that you should ask her out. Take the leap. What's the worst that can happen?"

Tamsin scoffed. "I could lose my job—again."

Eve shook her head. "This is a grown woman we're talking about. Someone who makes her own choices. Someone who's been dropping many a hint. The worst that can happen is that she'll say no, that's it."

"It's different when you live in a village like this. Word travels fast. If I ask her out and she says no, then tells a friend, and so on… Things can become really problematic for me."

"You've already had her over for dinner once. Invite her again. Don't say it's a date, just have one." Eve said it as though this was the brightest idea in the history of humankind.

"I'm not sure," Tamsin said.

"Of course you're not," Eve said, "But I'm here the rest of the weekend to help you change your mind."

CHAPTER SEVENTEEN

The sound of clapping drifted over to Diane as soon as she stepped out of her car. She locked it and walked out of her office car park. Instead of turning towards the entrance to the building, she headed for the village green, from where the cheering was coming.

Tynebury Spring Festival was one of the highlights on the village calendar. Part village fête, part flea market, it always brought together the villagers for a friendly baking competition and some trading of whatever had not survived the yearly spring clean. It even drew visitors from the surrounding villages.

Diane headed for the adult refreshment stall. Thompson & Partners always sponsored the stall by supplying the wine.

It was not even noon yet, but the few high tables that were set up under a gazebo were already packed with people enjoying a glass of wine. Thompson & Partners coasters were laid out on every table and Diane had found that this event always brought in one or two new clients. Apparently wine and accounting went pretty well together.

"Good morning, Stacey" she greeted her receptionist, who was manning the stall. "You're busy this morning."

"We've been swamped ever since we opened," she said. "Would you like a drink?"

"It's a bit early for me to start on the vino." Diane peered at the list that was displayed on the bar. "I'll have a sparkling grapefruit juice for now."

Stacey handed her the drink and Diane took it over to one of the tables to mingle. Even in a small village like Tynebury, networking was important.

She was in conversation with a local insurance broker, who brought in quite a bit of business for her, when she spotted a familiar figure browsing the second-hand book stall across from the bar.

Tamsin was examining paperback novels, taking one out, reading the back cover and putting it back in the display box.

Another woman came up to her, holding a larger book and showing it to Tamsin. They stood close together, shoulder to shoulder with their backs to Diane. Their laughter drifted over to her.

Was Tamsin out on another date already? She hadn't mentioned anything at dinner the other night. Maybe it hadn't been set up yet.

Or maybe Tamsin had sensed that Diane was not that interested in hearing about her dates. She would have been right about that, even though Diane could not really explain why. Or rather, she could, but was not ready to put it into words, even in her head.

The two women seemed quite close, much more so than people should be on a first date. So maybe it wasn't a first date, but a third or fourth.

How come Tamsin hadn't talked about someone she was seeing? The dinner had only been a week ago. Surely they could not have grown so close in such a short space of time.

Stop this, it's none of your business. Diane tried to tune back into the conversation between the two men standing next to her. Something about an insurance settlement after a house fire.

Her gaze was drawn towards Tamsin and her friend again. The other woman had turned slightly and Diane could see her face more clearly. She had very similar facial features to Tamsin, but her hair was different—longer and blonder. This must be the sister Tamsin had talked about.

Relief washed over Diane.

She thought back to last week, to the goodbye she and Tamsin had shared in the hallway of Tamsin's cottage, to the feeling of warmth and closeness that had engulfed her. And then she had gone and kissed Tamsin. Her mind had been lucid enough to go for her cheek, but in her heart, she knew that what she'd really wanted was to kiss Tamsin's lips.

What would it be like to feel Tamsin's lips on hers? She could still remember vividly the kiss she'd shared with Fiona decades ago, but somehow she knew that with Tamsin, it would be different. Less tentative, more passionate. She could almost feel Tamsin's mouth opening, their tongues meeting.

"Diane, what do you think?" A voice snapped her out of her reverie.

"Ehm, sorry," Diane said. "What were you saying?"

"Should the council grant the building permits for the new apartment block on Prairie Lane?" The insurance man was looking at her expectantly.

"I, er, I don't think they should," Diane said. "Will you excuse me, please?"

She stepped away from the table and walked over to the bar. It might still be early, but she could sure do with a glass of wine to wash away the images floating around her mind.

———

An hour later Diane was finishing her third glass of wine, now in the company of Isabelle, who had showed up determined to make a healthy contribution to the charitable causes the fete was supporting.

"Shall we have a wander around?" Isabelle had asked when she'd arrived. "I quite fancy some lemon drizzle cake for dessert tonight. And I spotted a vintage mirror that would fit perfectly in the guest room."

Diane had kept an eye on Tamsin and her sister, not wanting to have to face them in her current state of confusion. They had been browsing the stall manned by the local post office clerk, looking at her offerings of garden gnomes and other trinkets of doubtful taste.

"Let's have another drink first," Diane had replied, hoping Tamsin would have left by the time they finished their wine.

Isabelle had regarded her before saying, "All right. But just the one. You seem to be quite lubricated already."

Diane drank the last sip from her glass. She was experiencing a pleasant buzz, enhanced by the sun that had come out to bathe the village green in a beautiful spring light.

She scanned the assembled tents and stalls. Tamsin and her sister were nowhere to be seen. "Let's go for a browse." She took Isabelle's arm and they walked out towards the cake stall.

"The ladies of Tynebury have been very busy this year," Isabelle said, looking at the display of intricately decorated cakes. Each one was on some sort of arty display or pedestal, ready to be judged for the event's most coveted prize.

Diane's stomach rumbled at the sight. "Shall we get a slice to nibble on as we walk around?"

They each bought a piece of lemon drizzle cake and continued their exploration of the festival's offerings.

"How are Rob and Matthew?" Diane asked.

"They're fine. Looking at other clubs in the area where

being gay doesn't disqualify you from joining." There was obvious bitterness in Isabelle's tone of voice.

"Have you found out more about why Matthew was refused membership?"

"Stephen gave me a line about all available spots being taken by direct family of members, children and grandchildren, and that he should apply again next year. It's a load of crap, of course. The committee's stuck in the nineteen-fifties, that's what the issue is."

Diane thought for a moment. "Should we start a petition or something? Surely we can get a lot of prominent members to sign on. Everybody loves Rob and he's been a part of the club ever since he was born."

"I suppose we could," Isabelle said, "but I don't think it would do much good. They'll say they can't be prejudiced, since they just hired a gay pro."

This comment brought Tamsin to the front of Diane's mind again. Should she tell Isabelle about the feelings she'd been experiencing? Maybe her closest friend could give her some perspective and snap her out of this ridiculous infatuation.

"Speaking of," Isabelle exclaimed and pointed towards the end of the row of stalls.

Diane looked over and saw Tamsin and her sister walking towards them. *Damn.*

"Tamsin, hello." Isabelle kissed Tamsin on both cheeks. "We were just talking about you."

"I thought I could hear a ringing in my ears," Tamsin said. "Only good things, I hope."

Diane tried to think of something to say, but her mind was fuzzy from the wine and sun.

"This is my sister, Eve," Tamsin said. "Eve, these are two of the ladies from the golf club, Isabelle Avery and Diane Thompson."

HARPER & CAROLINE BLISS

Eve's gaze seemed to zoom in at the mention of Diane's name.

"Hello," Eve said, shaking Isabelle's hand. Then she took Diane's hand in both of hers and said, "I've heard so much about you."

Diane noticed how Tamsin's elbow bumped into her sister's arm. Eve let go of Diane's hand.

The power of speech still seemed to be eluding Diane. She knew she was supposed to reply something, but she just stood there in silence and nodded.

She felt Isabelle staring at her. "What's the matter, Diane? Cat got your tongue?"

"Sorry." At last, some words made it past Diane's lips. "I think I shouldn't have had that last glass of wine. I seem to have lost my manners." She addressed Tamsin's sister. "It's lovely to meet you, Eve."

Diane's gaze drifted back to Tamsin. She looked exquisite in a light blue fitted oxford shirt over a pair of dark jeans. She forced her eyes back up to the golf pro's face. "How are you, Tamsin? I've had another look at the documents you brought me last week. It seems pretty straightforward. You should make an appointment to go over everything. Maybe next week?" Stop babbling, she told herself.

Tamsin was looking at her in amusement, as if she could sense the turmoil going on inside Diane. "Sure, I'll call your office on Monday." She held Diane's gaze, until they heard a cough come from Eve.

Tamsin turned to her sister. Eve was giving her some kind of look and Diane saw her head nudge forward ever so slightly, seemingly in encouragement.

After another second or two Tamsin turned her head back to Diane and said, "Or maybe you could come over to mine for dinner again. I think I forgot to bring over some receipts. We could go over them with a glass of wine."

Diane's heart did a little tumble at the invitation. "That would be lovely, thank you." Diane's gaze moved down to Tamsin's mouth and again the thought of their lips meeting engulfed her. She tried to steer her mind towards her calendar for the coming week, but she drew a blank.

"I'll be in touch on Monday to set it up," Tamsin said, as if she could sense Diane's bewilderment. "We have to get going now. Bye, Isabelle."

Diane watched as Tamsin walked off with her sister. As they disappeared around the end of the aisle, Diane's eyes turned back to Isabelle, who was looking back at her with her mouth agape.

"Why are you looking at me like that?" Diane asked defensively.

Isabelle's eyes narrowed. "You're acting very strange, Diane Thompson. If I didn't know you better, the way you were giving her googly eyes, I'd think you have the hots for Ms Foxley."

"Don't be ridiculous," Diane waved off the suggestion. "As I said, too much wine, too early in the day." She grabbed hold of Isabelle's arm again and started walking. "Now let's go check out the flea market. Didn't you say there was a mirror you were interested in?"

CHAPTER EIGHTEEN

Tamsin looked in the mirror and threaded her fingers through her hair. She'd had her first really busy day at the club, teaching five hours back-to-back in the afternoon. Perhaps she should have picked another evening to have Diane over for dinner again, but the sensation she got in the pit of her stomach when she thought of Diane told her: no, tonight would do just fine.

She gave herself an encouraging smile, smoothed a stray strand of hair behind her ear, and nodded at herself. Eve's pep talk before she'd left on Sunday evening still lingered. "Flirt with her," her sister had said. "And see what happens. From what I've seen, Diane will be very receptive. The woman was practically speechless—stunned by your fine Foxley form— when we ran into her."

Tamsin had been forced to agree. Diane had behaved a little bizarrely. It reminded her of the other day in her hallway, when, kind of out of the blue, Diane had turned around and kissed her on the cheek.

The bell rang and Tamsin straightened her spine. Bramble was at the front door before she reached it, her tail wagging enthusiastically—expressing perfectly how Tamsin was feeling inside.

Tamsin ushered Diane in and they exchanged quick kisses on the cheek.

"Did you know the village next to Tynebury has a gin distillery? Not one of those new hipster ones, but one that's been there forever." She presented Tamsin with a bottle. "I brought you a sampling of their finest."

"You really shouldn't have." Tamsin took the bottle and, as she did, her finger slid against Diane's for a split second.

"Well, I wasn't going to arrive empty-handed, was I? You're a client." She sent Tamsin a smile. "And you know my hourly rate."

As they walked into the living room, Tamsin secretly hoped she was a little more than a client. The way Diane had just smiled at her, she figured she most likely was.

———

Tamsin had suggested they enjoy their drinks on the patio. It was a lovely spring evening—one that made her glad she was now living in the countryside, even though she'd spent most of her day outside already. It seemed to her that, now that it was in ample supply, Tamsin couldn't get enough of the fresh air and the endless buoyant greenery of Tynebury.

"Next time, you should really come to my house," Diane said, as she held up her gin and tonic. "That's twice you've invited me and I haven't returned the favour. That simply will not do."

"I very much look forward to seeing your house." Tamsin was glad for the smooth, cool liquid sliding down her throat when she drank. It offered her a much-needed moment of calm.

"It's a deal, then. Let's set it up soon." Diane's gaze lingered on hers, her blue eyes locking on Tamsin's over the rim of her cocktail glass. "Your sister seems like a lovely woman." Diane changed the subject and, with that, looked away.

"We're twins so I can't argue with that."

Diane arched up her eyebrows. "Really?"

"You couldn't tell?"

"You look alike, but I wouldn't have pegged you for twins."

"I know I look at least ten years younger than Eve. It's all that golf. Eve's cooped up inside most of the day. It makes all the difference."

"What does she do?"

"She illustrates books. Mainly children's books, although she's done a number of non-fiction ones as well."

"Interesting." Diane cocked her head. "Neither one of you has a traditional profession. No boring accountants in your family."

"My mother was a risk analyst for an insurance company, and that always seemed dreadfully boring to me."

Diane didn't say anything. The use of the word *was* when Tamsin mentioned her mother had the habit of halting a conversation.

"She died of cancer eight years ago," Tamsin filled the silence. "A tumour on her spine. One day, she had no idea it was there. The next day, she was told she only had a few months to live."

"I'm so sorry," Diane said, her voice warm.

Tamsin drank so she didn't have to speak for a while. Over the years, she'd tried to steel herself to handle the inevitable moments her mother popped up in conversation, but it had never quite worked.

"My father's a furniture maker. Bring the man a piece of wood and he'll make you a chair out of it. At the very least." Tamsin smiled at the thought of her dad.

"That's a very artistic family you have." Diane's eyes had

narrowed. "Did they, um, take it well when you… came out of the closet?"

"I can't complain." Tamsin shrugged. "I think they'd guessed already, but it was still an adjustment when I actually said it out loud for the first time. But it was never too big a deal." Tamsin's coming out was long behind her and she barely thought of it. Having a parent die had changed her family's history and her telling them that she was a lesbian had become one of those small, almost insignificant things that had once occurred but didn't raise any more eyebrows. "How about Isabelle? How did she react when her son came out?"

Diane chuckled. "You can never tell Rob this, of course, but I knew he was gay long before he did. Isabelle told me of her suspicions when he was only twelve or thirteen, I think. So it was hardly a shock when he did finally tell her."

"She didn't have any trouble accepting it?" Tamsin inquired.

"Not that I know of and I've known Isabelle all my life. We both grew up here. Isabelle's husband took a bit longer to come around, if I remember correctly, but being gay is… almost ordinary these days, isn't it?"

Tamsin drew up her eyebrows. "Almost ordinary?"

"As in that it doesn't make that much difference." Diane's cheeks grew pink. She grabbed her glass off the table and seemed to hide her face behind it.

"Speaking from personal experience, I can tell you that to many people it still makes a big difference. And I've been"—she made air quotes with her fingers—"'lucky', I guess. There's no such thing as true equality yet. That will take a few more generations of increasingly open-minded people, but we'll get there in the end." Tamsin didn't much feel like getting too political. She did her best not to be offended by Diane's words, who was obviously regretting them, what with the way she was knocking back the rest of her cocktail, her glance skittering from here to there.

"I didn't mean to imply anything," Diane said after she'd taken a breath. "I do hope you haven't experienced any discrimination in Tynebury."

"Not that I'm aware of, although I'm sure my sexual orientation has been discussed behind my back."

Diane put her glass down again. "Truthfully," she tilted her head slightly, "yes, it has been talked about. When a stranger moves into the village, tongues will invariably wag."

"It's to be expected." Tamsin emptied her drink. "Shall we get the dull part over with and have a look at my accounts before we eat?"

"Gladly." Diane seemed relieved.

Tamsin grinned at her, wanting Diane to feel comfortable. After all, Tamsin had been having conversations like this all of her life and would probably keep on having them for as long as she lived. For Diane, things were probably a little different.

A warm glow spread through Tamsin's core as she escorted Diane inside.

———

After a long day on the golf course, Tamsin had kept the meal simple and had grilled chicken and asparagus. Yet, Diane had savoured every bite of the dish as though it was a Michelin-starred offering.

"That was one of the things that threw me the most after the divorce," Diane said. "Having to cook for one." She shook her head. "I always got my portions wrong, as though simply cutting the amount of ingredients in half was impossible." She smiled at Tamsin. "It'll be a delight to cook for you. Shall we say next weekend?"

"Sure. I have to go to London on Friday for a big family dinner, but I can do Saturday or Sunday." Tamsin had to remind herself that, in her head, this was a date. And as far as dates went, to have the next one lined up already before the end of the first, was a definite success. The only problem, of course, was that Diane might not see it as a date at all, but simply as an opportunity to thank Tamsin for her hospitality— and the pleasure of cooking for two instead of one.

"It's a date," Diane said then.

Tamsin gave herself an imaginary high-five. "Can I ask you a personal question?"

"I think we've reached that stage." Diane sipped from her water. She'd barely touched the white wine Tamsin had served with dinner, claiming the gin had gone straight to her head. Tamsin had followed her example and drank mainly water. It was a good opportunity to gauge her feelings for Diane without the effects of alcohol.

"Since Lawrence, have you never got involved with anyone else?"

Diane pursed her lips, then shook her head. "You may have noticed that single men of a certain age are in short supply. To put it really bluntly, members of the opposite sex seem to kick the bucket much earlier than us. Add to that the cliché males of the species who, once in the throes of middle age, leave their spouse for a younger model, and it's the classic example of a scarcity situation." She chuckled. "Every single time a man becomes a widower, I've seen him snapped up quick as lightning." She sighed theatrically. "It's truly a sight to behold, the way some of my friends behave. After a certain age, when it comes to things like that, all sense of decorum just seems to disappear."

Tamsin couldn't help but chuckle. "Now that you mention it. I do remember an instance when one of the male members of my previous club lost his wife... The poor guy was all but swarmed every time he showed up."

"I bet he didn't remain single for very long," Diane said

wistfully. "Just another example of the great inequality between men and women."

"That's at least one advantage of being a lesbian then," Tamsin said. "The war between the sexes has always completely passed me by."

"There's definitely something to be said for that." Diane shot her a smile that Tamsin couldn't quite decipher. It was different to her ordinary, full-wattage smile and was unaccompanied by her usual hooting laugh.

Eve's words rang in her ears. *Flirt a little.*

"Have you heard of the term *latebian*?" Tamsin asked. "Some claim that the shortage of men of a certain age may very well have something to do with it, although, I for one, refuse to believe that."

Diane's cheeks grew pink again. "I—er, as a matter of fact, I am familiar with that word."

"Then you know what I'm getting at." Tamsin looked Diane straight in the eye.

Despite her reddening cheeks, Diane's returning stare didn't waver. "I'm not sure that I do."

Now or never, Tamsin thought. The moment had been brewing for a while, and if she didn't seize it now, she feared she might never. She rose from her chair and said, "Stay right where you are." She walked over to Diane, looked her in the eye again, relished the sparkling, delicious heat that swarmed through her body, and leaned in.

CHAPTER NINETEEN

Diane's gaze followed Tamsin as she stood and walked to Diane's side of the dining table. Tamsin stopped and leaned in towards her. Tamsin's intense stare was illuminated with a passion Diane had not seen directed at her in a long time.

Tamsin halted her approach when her face was just a couple of inches away from Diane's and put her hands on Diane's shoulders.

Tamsin's gaze moved down to Diane's mouth. Her intention was perfectly clear, but she seemed to be waiting for Diane to take the final step, to bridge the last remaining distance between their lips.

As if pushed by an external force, Diane's head moved towards Tamsin's. In her mind she could hear a voice saying: *What are you doing? This is not how Diane Thompson behaves.* But her mind did not seem to have any control over her body.

She closed her eyes and pursed her lips. As she finally made contact with Tamsin's mouth, warmth spread across her cheeks. She leaned in a little more, pressing her lips more firmly against Tamsin's, and the heat started making its way down her chest.

Tamsin pulled back and Diane opened her eyes again. The passion Diane had seen in Tamsin's stare before seemed to have increased in intensity.

"Do you understand what I'm getting at now?" Tamsin asked, a small smile on her lips.

Diane only managed a small nod. Of course she'd known from the moment Tamsin had said *latebian*. She felt like she ought to stand, so Tamsin could stop hovering over her, but her legs were incapable of any movement, her backside glued to her chair.

"Did I read the situation correctly?" Tamsin continued.

Diane opened her mouth to answer but no sound came out. Inside her, two voices were warring. The one from earlier kept repeating *no, no, no.* But another, more assured voice was saying: *yes, you certainly did.*

After a couple of silent seconds had passed Diane realised she needed to show some kind of reaction to Tamsin's question. She managed to regain some control over her body and took hold of Tamsin's hands. She rose from her chair and found herself standing so close to Tamsin, their bodies were almost touching.

Diane kept her gaze glued to Tamsin's and instead of answering, she leaned in towards her, bringing their mouths together once more. Diane opened hers slightly and let her tongue gently touch Tamsin's lips. They parted immediately and Tamsin's tongue met hers in a slow, languorous dance.

The warmth consuming her now descended even lower, pooling in a ball of fire at her very core. How long had it been since she'd experienced this?

Tamsin moved her hands from Diane's grasp and placed them on either side of Diane's face. She pulled her in even closer, as their tongues intensified their pace.

Diane brought her hands to Tamsin's sides, where her top had ridden up slightly and Diane's fingers made contact with skin. She felt how the surface instantly changed to goose bumps.

While Diane was baffled by what she was experiencing, she was even more astounded by the effect she appeared to be having on Tamsin. She could not remember the last time the touch of her fingers had provoked such an immediate reaction in someone.

Their kiss slowed and Tamsin pulled her mouth away from Diane's. "I've been wanting to kiss you for quite some time," Tamsin said, her voice almost a whisper.

"B—but," Diane stammered. Her mind went blank.

The confusion must have been visible on her face, because Tamsin took hold of her hand and said, "Come, let's sit on the sofa and talk. We'll be more comfortable there."

Tamsin led Diane to the sofa and gently pushed her down before taking a seat next to her, leaving a small space between them. She still held Diane's hand.

With her other hand Tamsin gently touched Diane's face and turned it towards her. "What are you thinking right now?" she asked.

Diane could not bring herself to look Tamsin in the eye. She pulled her hand from Tamsin's and started fidgeting with the button of her blouse. "I, er," she started. Where her mind had been blank before, it was now a whirlwind of questions and emotions that swirled around so much, she couldn't grasp a single one. "I don't know," she just managed to say.

"Why don't you take a few deep breaths," Tamsin said. "I find that usually helps to bring some order to my thoughts."

Diane inhaled as deep as she could before letting the air out slowly. Her breath trembled. Another deep inhale and a more deliberate exhale. As if by magic, the tempest in her head slowed and as she continued to focus on her breathing a single thought came to the forefront, leaving the others behind.

"I've been wanting to kiss you too." She looked up towards Tamsin now and held her gaze. "Although I don't know what it means, or what I should do."

Tamsin sent her a warm smile. "I understand it must be confusing for you. It is for me too."

"How so?" Diane asked. Surely Tamsin was used to kissing other women.

"When I moved here, I made myself the promise to not get involved with anyone at the club. I didn't want a repeat of what had happened at Chalstone." Tamsin paused for a moment. "Please don't take this the wrong way, but I've never had these kinds of feelings for someone like you, Diane."

"Someone like me?" Diane was taken aback. "Someone old, you mean?"

"No, no," Tamsin quickly responded. "I mean someone so accomplished and interesting. Someone I look up to." She thought for a moment. "I suppose it might have something to do with you having more life experience, but that's not all it is. In my previous relationships I was always the stronger one—that's one way of putting it. The one who was looked up to, depended on. And I liked being in that position. But with you, I feel like the roles are reversed. And it's quite scary, to be honest."

Diane was, again, at a loss for words. She felt flattered in a way by Tamsin's declaration, but it did nothing to diminish her confusion. As much as she wanted to stay and repeat the kiss they had exchanged in the dining room, she felt she needed to gather herself more, and she would not be able to do so in Tamsin's company.

"I think I should leave." Diane stood.

Tamsin rose as well. "Don't you think we should talk some more?"

Diane took Tamsin's hands in hers. "We do, I agree. Please don't feel I'm ignoring what you just said." She took another deep breath. "I need some time to get my head around this. Will you give it to me?"

Tamsin nodded, but Diane couldn't help but notice a hint of sadness in her eyes.

Diane leaned forward and gave Tamsin a gentle kiss on the lips. "We'll talk soon, I promise."

She bent to pick up her bag and walked to the hallway door. There she turned around and looked at Tamsin, who was still standing in the same spot. The sight filled her with the same warmth she'd felt before.

"Good night," Diane said, and walked out into the hallway. She quickly made her way to her car.

Before starting the engine, she took a moment and closed her eyes, recalling the sensation of Tamsin's tongue in her mouth. She had so many questions for Tamsin and herself, but there was one thing she couldn't deny.

She hadn't felt this alive in years.

———

Diane tapped her fingers on her desk nervously as she waited for Isabelle to pick up the phone. She had barely slept after the dinner at Tamsin's and what had happened. She had already downed three cups of coffee since arriving at the office an hour ago.

"Hello, Isabelle speaking," the voice on the other end of the line announced.

"It's me," Diane said. "Are you busy today? I need to speak with you."

"Well hello to you too." Isabelle gave a chuckle.

"Sorry. *Hello.* Are you free?"

"As a matter of fact I am," Isabelle said. "I was just on my way into the village to do some shopping. Should I pop into your office first?"

"Yes, please do. See you soon." Diane disconnected the call, not even waiting for Isabelle's reply.

Fifteen minutes later Isabelle knocked on the open door of Diane's office and walked right in.

"What on earth is the matter with you?" Isabelle asked before she'd even sat down. "You sounded like you were on speed or something when you called."

Diane got up and closed the door. She took a seat on the other side of her desk, next to Isabelle.

"Something happened last night," Diane started. "Something I can't quite wrap my head around." She fell silent then, unsure of how to tell her friend what she had done. What if she turned out to be disgusted or horrified and didn't want anything more to do with Diane?

"Well," Isabelle said expectantly. "What is it? You look like you're about to confess to a murder." She paused, frowning. "You haven't killed anyone, have you?"

"Don't be ridiculous," Diane said, waving off her comment. "I, er… Lately I've been feeling things I haven't felt before. Or things I haven't felt in a long time. Romantic things."

"Diane," Isabelle exclaimed. "That's great. Why are you looking so grim, then?"

Diane swallowed hard and steeled herself for what she was about to say. She was looking down at her hands which were clutched together tightly. "Here's the thing. The person I've been having these feelings for, well, they're not who you'd expect." She paused and looked up to meet Isabelle's stare. "This person is a woman."

"A woman," Isabelle said flatly. She seemed to ponder this for a moment then said, "Who?" She brought her hand to her mouth in mock drama. "It's not me, is it?"

Diane burst out laughing. "I love you dearly, but not in that way." She became serious again. "It's Tamsin. And it seems she has been experiencing the same kind of feelings for me."

"I see," Isabelle said.

"You don't seem surprised." Diane had expected a stronger reaction from her friend.

"I saw you two interact at the festival," Isabelle said pensively. "There was something about it. I had a suspicion—I even told you. Now it all makes sense."

"Last night I went over to hers for dinner and, well... she kissed me." Diane looked down at her hands again. "And I kissed her back," she said quietly.

Isabelle leaned forward in her chair. "How did it feel?"

Diane sighed and looked up at Isabelle, her lips forming into a smile. "It was mind-blowing. Like nothing I've ever experienced before."

"This is great news." Isabelle took Diane's hands in hers. "Isn't it?" She looked at Diane questioningly.

"I don't know," Diane said. "What can come of it? We can hardly date, can we? I mean, I'm Diane Thompson, fifty-four year old accountant, heterosexual as far as I know. What would people think?"

"Who cares about that?" Isabelle looked at her intently. "Anyway, I think you're getting ahead of yourself a little there. In my view, the only question is: do you want to kiss her again? And, you know..." Isabelle waggled her eyebrows at this.

Diane scoffed. "Stop it. I haven't even thought about that."

Isabelle gave her a sceptic look. "I sincerely doubt that. How long has it been since the divorce? And how long had it been since you and Lawrence had done the deed before that? I know you're a woman of a certain age, but surely your body's still capable of feeling the flames of passion."

Diane laughed at this. "Okay, I admit, the thought has crossed my mind. And my body is very much capable of feeling passion, thank you very much." She paused. "What should I do,

Isabelle? I'm completely confused right now, I need some advice from my oldest friend. I invited Tamsin for dinner at mine on Saturday—this was before the kissing—and now I'm not sure if I should go through with it."

Isabelle sat up straight in her chair and took on a serious expression. "As your oldest friend, my advice is this"—she held up one finger—"you should definitely have Tamsin over for dinner on Saturday. You invited her and it would be rude to cancel. One thing you're decidedly not is rude." A second finger joined the first one. "You should kiss her again. If only to make sure the first time wasn't a fluke."

"But—"

"—I'm not finished." Isabelle held up a third finger. "Lastly, if she's agreeable to it, you should let her shag you senseless."

Diane's mouth fell open.

"You asked for my advice," Isabelle said. "That's it." She stood up and leaned forward to peck Diane on the cheek. "Now I have to go shopping. Ted's home for lunch and I have nothing in the fridge." She walked to the door and opened it. Before leaving she turned towards Diane. "Close your mouth dear, it's not becoming for a lady of your class."

Diane sat in the same position for a while after Isabelle had left, as if glued to the chair. Isabelle's words kept reverberating in her head. *Shag you senseless*. When had anyone ever said something so crass to her? More importantly, why did the words fill Diane with such a sense of excitement and anticipation that she wished she could instantly transport herself to Saturday?

CHAPTER TWENTY

Tamsin still hadn't heard from Diane. As on most Thursdays, there was a Ladies' Day competition at the club, and she couldn't help but wonder if Diane would show up. Maybe it would all depend on the progress she was making with the end of the fiscal year—or, perhaps even more so, on her desire to run into Tamsin.

Tamsin was teaching Debbie that afternoon and afterwards she had a meeting with the club's secretary. The odds of bumping into Diane were greater than on any other day that week and she was hoping that she would—if only to break the tension that had been building in her gut, cramping up her muscles. Tamsin could hardly teach Debbie how to relax into her swing when she herself was as stiff as a plank. This business with Diane was affecting her work life, that's what it came down to. It had to be dealt with swiftly.

She walked around the grounds with her ears perked up and her eyes scanning her surroundings. She sat on the bench overlooking the practice area, waiting for Debbie. It would take a whole bunch of lessons before the poor woman could hit a ball somewhat decently. She just didn't have the instinct for hitting the ball the right way. But she was eager, and that made up for a lot. And her husband had deep pockets and, it would appear, was determined for his second wife to master golf as well as his first.

She heard footsteps approach and got ready to push any thought of Diane from her head, at least for the duration of this lesson. She owed all of her pupils her full attention.

Tamsin turned around and, instead of Debbie heading towards the driving range, Diane was walking in her direction.

"I ran into Debbie in the car park. She's only just arrived," Diane said matter-of-factly. "I figured she had a lesson planned with you, so…" She left the last word hanging, as though it held some deeper meaning. "I wanted to have a quick word." Diane glanced around. "About the other night." She put her hands in her trouser pockets, then pulled them back out. "I'm sorry I rushed off like that. I was just so terribly confused. I didn't really know what to do. Running seemed like the best option at the time." She smiled sheepishly.

Tamsin rose from the bench but kept her distance from Diane. "It's okay. I understand. It's a somewhat confusing situation." The urge to press her lips to Diane's again rose quickly to the surface.

"Will you still come to dinner on Saturday?" Diane smiled wider—all sheepishness gone. The sight of it relaxed some of Tamsin's tensed-up muscles.

"Of course," Tamsin said. "I'm looking forward to it already." Tamsin glanced at the path stretched out behind Diane and saw Debbie rounding the corner. "Debbie's on her way." She witnessed how Diane's demeanour shifted, how her glance transformed from warm to guarded again.

"I'll leave you to it." Diane's tone was clipped and the obvious change in her twisted something in Tamsin's stomach. But they'd had this moment together, and it had taken away some of Tamsin's anguish.

Before she turned around, Diane said, "I'll text you my address."

Tamsin nodded and watched her scoot off, giving Debbie the most imperceptible of nods. The contrast between them couldn't be bigger. Diane looked like the women Tamsin had encountered in golf clubs all her life. Elegantly dressed, head held high, shoulders back, that gait that spelled gravitas. Debbie, with her long faux-blonde ponytail tucked through the back of her garish designer cap and too-bright attire, stuck out like a sore thumb in an old-fashioned club like this.

"Hi, Tamsin." She greeted Tamsin with a kiss on the cheek as though they were friends. "Did Diane want an update on my progress?" Tamsin couldn't fault her sense of humour, however. And she knew all about feeling like an outsider.

"I told her you're making swift strides," Tamsin said. "And that you'll be beating her in no time."

"As if." Debbie slipped her hand into her golfing glove. "But I'll keep on trying."

———

"It would be lovely if you could come up as well," Eve said. "An entire week in the Derbyshire countryside might be a bit much for little old me."

They were having dinner at Lomax, their father's favourite restaurant in London, which was nothing more than a glorified pub. But Tamsin had to admit that the lamb was delicious.

"I can only come on the weekend," Tamsin said. "And even that might be tricky."

Eve curled up her upper lip, the way she'd done as long as Tamsin could remember.

"Unlike yours, my job is very much location-dependent, you know that." Tamsin glanced at her sister, who probably knew very well that Tamsin couldn't just take a week off to keep her company while she experimented with transferring illustrations onto their father's furniture. "Even though what you want to do excites me no end."

Eve cocked her head.

"I'm serious," Tamsin said.

"Are you working on anything yourself, Tazzie?" their father asked, having only just extricated himself from a conversation with James about his life insurance. Their mother had always taken care of all things financial and James had gallantly stepped in after she'd passed away—neither Tamsin, nor Eve had felt equipped to do so.

"I managed to get my hands on a chest of drawers from the fifties," Tamsin said. "I'm thinking of doing it up with wallpaper. I have just the print in mind."

"Email me before and after pictures," their dad said. He wasn't the type to make Tamsin feel bad for not dropping by as often as before, now that she had her own workspace at home—and she'd been busy with moving house. But they'd strengthened their bond over their joint love for old furniture and Tamsin made a mental note to drive up to Derbyshire on her next two consecutive days off. Maybe next weekend. This made her think of the upcoming weekend and her date with Diane. Dinner with her family was no time to consider what might happen, even though a bevy of butterflies ignited storm after storm in her belly.

"I was doodling the other day," Eve said, "just after you told me about doing up that chest of drawers with wallpaper, and I came up with a great design." Eve reached for her purse. "Let me show you."

The next half hour was spent discussing Eve's design, their dad having the loudest opinion of all, and discussing ways of getting it printed. James even got out his phone and started doing research on the spot. It ended with Tamsin promising to use some of Eve's not-yet-existing wallpaper on the next piece of furniture she worked on.

"Wouldn't it be fun if we could all work together," Eve said. "You and dad could build the furniture. I could make it look funky. And James, well…" She glanced at her husband. "You can make sure we make enough money."

"How about I remain gainfully employed instead?" He shot Eve a wide smile.

"Ever since last weekend in Tynebury, I've been dreaming of a life in the country," Eve said.

"We can get a weekend home. Somewhere in between Derbyshire and Tynebury. The best of both worlds," James, ever the peacemaker, said.

"That sounds like music to my ears," Eve said.

"Wonderful, then I can stay at your place in London while you're away," Tamsin said.

Her sister slapped her on the knee. "No way. If I'm escaping to the country of a weekend, I want you there."

"I'm just glad Tynebury has inspired you," Tamsin said. "Who would have thought?"

"She'll be wanting a dog next," James said.

"Bramble adores me," Eve said.

Tamsin leaned back and watched them bicker playfully. These three people were her closest family and having them together in one spot brought her great joy. For a brief moment, she allowed herself to wonder how Diane would fit into this foursome. What would her dad make of her? And vice versa? Then she pushed the thought of Diane from her mind—again— and rejoined the conversation.

When Tamsin excused herself to use the ladies' room, Eve rose and followed her.

"Are you ready for your hot date tomorrow?" she asked.

Tamsin was glad that, at least, she hadn't asked that partic- ular question in front of their father. There was no need to get his hopes up of Tamsin meeting someone 'suitable', as he put it. Not that he ever asked her many questions about her love life—that had been firmly her mother's department.

"Ready as I can be." Tamsin had told Eve on the phone about the kiss. After all, her sister had been the one to encourage her to go for it.

"Hey." Eve put a hand on her shoulder. "You deserve some happiness."

"Doesn't everyone?" A thought popped into Tamsin's head —another one inspired by Diane. "Do you ever think dad will find someone else?" From the way Diane had described it, her father must be considered a most eligible bachelor.

"He's not exactly looking for it, I think," Eve said. "And it would be weird."

"Try to find out what you can when you're staying with him." It dawned on Tamsin that the age difference between her and Diane was almost the same as between Diane and her father. In fact, for a man like her father to start something with a woman of Diane's age would be considered perfectly normal —the other way around, probably not so much.

"Way to change the subject, Taz," Eve said. "You'd best call me on Sunday. Unless, of course, your lips are too busy kissing Diane's."

Tamsin elbowed her sister in the side. "Don't you have to pee?" she asked. "Because that's the real reason I came in here." As she entered the stall, Tamsin considered that, when she had been dating Ellen, her sister had never shown the same enthusiasm for finding out all the details about their tryst.

CHAPTER TWENTY-ONE

Diane had been standing in front of her open wardrobe for about five minutes. For the third time she slid the hangers with blouses and tops from one side of the bar to the other, one at a time.

Nothing she owned seemed appropriate for a dinner date with a woman she had kissed and was considering seeing more of. It seemed pretty unbelievable, considering the number of clothes in her wardrobe.

She took out a dark blue blouse, with a stiff collar and long sleeves. *This isn't a work dinner, you don't want to look like an accountant.* Next was a white top with a frilly edge on the sleeves and collar. Diane considered it for a second, but then hung it back on the bar. Too grandmother-ish. Which, she reminded herself, was what she was going to become quite soon. A grandmother.

This filled her with a slight panic. What kind of grandmother starts dating a woman for the first time? And why would anyone want to date a soon-to-be grandmother?

Stop this. Diane shook herself out of the spiral of negative thoughts. She was not a grandmother, yet. And Tamsin did not appear to have any issue at all with that aspect of Diane.

She finally decided on a light blue V-neck knit top. It was cut quite deep, admittedly, but if she couldn't show off a bit of cleavage on this date, then when could she?

Diane sat in front of the mirror and inspected her face. The slight bags under her eyes betrayed the sleepless nights she'd been having, drafting all kinds of scenarios in her head about how the evening would unfold. Should she wear some make-up? Wasn't a date about looking one's best and seducing the other? Tamsin never seemed to wear any, but then Tamsin had the healthy complexion of someone who spends most of their days outside.

Diane picked up her mascara, but found there was a slight tremor in her hand. She'd never be able to apply any make-up in a proper manner with her nerves acting up like this. *Au naturel* it was, then.

As Diane was walking down the stairs, the doorbell rang. Goodness, Tamsin was punctual.

Diane went over to the front door, her heart beating furiously in her chest. She paused for a second to take a deep breath and steady herself, and then opened the door.

Before her stood someone she assumed was Tamsin, holding up a huge potted plant with budding purple flowers in front of her face.

"Hello," Tamsin said from behind the plant. "I wasn't sure if you preferred flowers or plants, but I figured this would look nice in any garden."

"It's gorgeous," Diane said opening the door wide and making way for Tamsin to come inside.

Tamsin immediately deposited the pot on the hallway table. "I ordered it online and picked it up on my walk over," she said shaking out her arms, "but they didn't say how heavy it was on the website. It weighs a ton." She turned to Diane and a warm smile lit up her face. "It's so lovely to see you." She took a step closer and leaned forward to brush a kiss over Diane's lips.

Where Diane's heart had been beating furiously with nerves a minute ago, it was now doing a somersault at the touch of Tamsin's kiss. She put her hands on Tamsin's shoulders and pulled her closer, pressing her lips more firmly against Tamsin's.

She let go after a few seconds, not wanting to get too carried away this early in the evening. "I'm so happy you're here," she said. "Please, come through." She led them into the living room. She had tried sitting outside on the patio earlier, but it had been chilly, so she had set up a couple of glasses and some nibbles on the low table in front of the sofa.

Tamsin walked around the large lounge, looking at the art on the walls. "This place is amazing." She stopped in front of the sideboard and leaned forward to look at the array of picture frames, mostly candid shots of Timothy: as a child, at his graduation, with Lucy at their wedding.

She turned around to Diane and said, "Sorry, I don't mean to snoop around like this. I just love looking at the more personal things people display in their homes." She had a mischievous sparkle in her eyes. "Is this your son?" she asked pointing at one of the frames.

"Yes," Diane said, "that's Timothy." Diane couldn't help a smile from forming on her face at the mention of her lovely boy.

"I can't wait to meet him," Tamsin said, straightening her posture again.

Diane froze. She hadn't even thought about having to introduce Tamsin to Timothy if things progressed.

"Sorry," Tamsin said quickly and placed her hand on Diane's arm. "I'm getting way ahead of myself."

"What can I get you to drink?" Diane asked, steering the

conversation onto more comfortable ground. "I have some white wine in the fridge."

"White wine would be perfect."

Diane took her time opening the bottle and placing it in an ice bucket. When she returned to the lounge Tamsin had taken a seat on the sofa, her right leg slung over her left and her arms stretched out on the back rest.

She looked so comfortable, as if she belonged in Diane's home.

Diane put the bucket on the table and took out the bottle to pour out the drinks. As she handed Tamsin her glass, Tamsin's index finger touched her thumb and gave it a light brush. Tamsin was looking straight into Diane's eyes and the combination of her touch and stare sent shivers up Diane's spine.

Diane sat down next to Tamsin on the sofa. "So," she said.

Tamsin was still peering at her. "Here we are."

Diane could not take the intensity of Tamsin's stare and looked down at her glass. She took a sip, and then another. She felt like she should start things off, as it were, since they were in her home and she was the one who had run off the previous time.

She cleared her throat. "I've been thinking about you a lot since we had dinner at your place. As a matter of fact, if I wasn't doing someone's year end accounts, I was probably thinking about you." She finally looked up at Tamsin.

Tamsin's face was a picture of openness and attention. Her green eyes exuded kindness and sympathy. But also something else. Something that spurred Diane on.

"I thought a lot about the kiss we shared, and what it means." Diane paused. "I, er—I talked about it with Isabelle. I hope you don't mind." She recalled Isabelle's advice of a few days ago.

Tamsin took Diane's hand in hers. "What did Isabelle have

to say?" Tamsin's fingers were softly rubbing the back of Diane's hand.

Diane put her glass down on the table. "Isabelle said I should do this." She took a deep breath and put her hand on Tamsin's cheek. She pulled Tamsin's head in towards hers and gently kissed her on the lips. After a while she opened her mouth a fraction, allowing Tamsin's tongue to meet hers. As their kiss gained in intensity, all the worries that had occupied Diane's mind—about her age, about how Timothy would react —seemed to disappear and the only emotions that remained were happiness, and a desire for more.

When they came up for air, Tamsin said, "I've always liked Isabelle." She smiled at Diane. "Did she say anything else?"

Diane chuckled. "She did, but I'm not sure I'm ready to implement that advice just yet." Diane had spent a lot of time going over that part of the equation in her head. She considered herself a pretty well-educated woman, who knew the mechanics of what could happen between two women. But when the time came, would she be able to overcome her fears and be intimate with Tamsin? And how would Tamsin react to having a fifty-four-year-old body in front of her, she who was used to sleeping with women thirty years younger?

"You've been on my mind too, Diane." Tamsin had a solemn look on her face. "I know all of this is confusing to you. It was a long time ago, but I remember how it felt to realise that I had feelings for a girl. It was terrifying and exciting at the same time. Of course, I can't pretend to know exactly how you're experiencing it, but I think I have an idea." She was still holding Diane's hand. "I want to spend more time with you. I want to get to know you, explore this thing we have between us."

"I want that too," Diane said, holding on to Tamsin's hand tightly. "After I left your place the other night, I felt so energised and alive. I haven't felt that way in years. And I want to feel like that again." The passion in her own voice surprised

Diane. She couldn't remember the last time she'd been so invigorated.

Tamsin's face broke out into a warm smile. "You can't imagine how happy I am to hear that." She pulled Diane into her arms, hugging her tightly.

The feeling of Tamsin's embrace started a fire in the pit of Diane's stomach. Her body seemed to awaken from a long hibernation and she felt its longing for touch and intimacy in every fibre of her being.

Diane extricated herself from Tamsin's arms and stood. She held out her hands to Tamsin and pulled her up out of the sofa. "I feel as though if I don't do this now, I might lose my nerve." She looked down at her feet for a moment, then moved her gaze back up to meet Tamsin's. "I'm ready to do what Isabelle told me to do." She pulled Tamsin closer against her and gave her a languorous kiss. "Will you come upstairs with me?"

Tamsin's eyes were alight with a fire more intense than Diane had ever seen. They were reflecting Diane's desire right back at her. "Are you sure?" Tamsin asked.

Diane just nodded and pulled Tamsin in for another kiss.

CHAPTER TWENTY-TWO

Tamsin opened her eyes. She felt something scratchy between her right shoulder blade and the bed sheets. She pushed herself up and glanced over her shoulder. A crumb.

Diane had brought them up a few slices of toast to nibble on last night, which had been the extent of their dinner.

Diane. Where was she?

Tamsin looked around the room. To her right, the curtains had been drawn over a small window. To her left, a chair had Tamsin's clothes draped over its back. Underneath the sheets, Tamsin was naked. They had really done this. Tamsin had just woken up in Diane Thompson's bed, only... Diane was nowhere to be seen.

She listened for sounds in the house. Maybe Diane had gone down the stairs to fetch more toast, famished from making love—and missing dinner. In her own house, the first sound Tamsin usually heard was Bramble rousing from sleep. This house was eerily quiet. No clanking of cups. No smell of coffee drifting upwards.

Had last night freaked Diane out so much she'd done a runner again? From her own house?

Tamsin scratched her head. There wasn't much else for her to do than get up and put her clothes back on. Bramble needed to be fed and let out. At least her dog would be happy to see her this morning.

Tamsin threw off the sheets and slipped into her jeans and blouse. She walked to the window and opened the curtains. The window looked out over Diane's back garden and the rolling landscape beyond. Then all the images from last night flooded Tamsin's mind. The kiss on the sofa. Diane's outstretched hand. The rush up the stairs, followed by tearing off each other's clothes. Tamsin had been gentle with Diane, careful and deliberate. Perhaps not careful enough. She took a deep breath, turned on her heel, and headed downstairs, where she found no one.

She had just located her handbag and was about to swing it over her shoulder, when she heard a car approach. She stilled to listen further. The dull thud of a car door being shut. The click-clack of heels on the driveway. The scratching of keys in the front door lock.

Tamsin peeked her head into the hallway and looked into Diane's face. She was holding a paper bag from which emanated the most enticing smell.

"You're up," Diane said.

"You're *here*," Tamsin replied.

"Where else would I be?" Diane closed the door behind her and walked up to Tamsin.

"I thought you'd run off again." Tamsin identified the smell coming from the bag as freshly baked croissants. She could murder one of those.

"From my own house?" Diane turned on her full-wattage smile.

Tamsin shrugged.

"I'd been awake for two hours and you just kept on sleeping. I took the opportunity to get us some much-needed breakfast.

I left you a note by the coffee machine." She held up the bag. "Are you hungry?"

"Desperately." Tamsin planted her hands on Diane's hips and pulled her close. "Someone made me miss dinner last night." She shook her head. "What kind of a dinner party is that?"

"The hostess deserves all the punishment you can muster, but first," Diane leaned in, "she also deserves a kiss."

Diane smelled freshly showered, her breath minty. Tamsin felt a little self-conscious, but they'd slept together last night, so she kissed her despite feeling less than fresh. The way she leaned into the kiss, Diane didn't seem to mind at all.

"Coffee," Diane whispered, when they broke from their kiss. "And lots of it."

"Maybe I should jump in the shower first," Tamsin offered.

"Nonsense." Diane glanced at the bag of croissants. "If I don't eat in the next minute, I'm not sure what I'll do. Isabelle told me that 'hangry' is very much a thing these days." Diane led the way to the kitchen.

Tamsin eagerly followed her. In her previous affairs, she'd always been the one running out to buy pastries in the morning. It was nice to have it done for her.

Diane made coffee while Tamsin laid the table and then they sat next to each other at the kitchen table which offered the same view as the bedroom window, only much grander.

Tamsin bit into the croissant. She'd had croissants from the same bakery before but they'd never tasted like this. It wasn't just that she was hungry. It was the woman sitting next to her, sharing breakfast with her.

"Good god." Diane moaned in exaggerated fashion. "Where have you been all my life?"

"Are you talking about me?" Tamsin asked. "Because I grew up in Derbyshire, then I moved to South London, although when I say South London, I actually mean Croydon. Then I

HARPER & CAROLINE BLISS

moved to Tynebury and here I finally am." She turned to face Diane.

Diane's gaze on her was soft. Her eyes narrowed further when she spoke. "Last night was amazing." She paused. "I feel like a different person. Like a new me."

"Your latebian status isn't freaking you out too much?"

Diane shook her head. "Not one bit, which is a bit strange. I might still be under the influence of… sex with Tamsin Foxley." She curved her lips into an irresistible smile.

Tamsin waggled her eyebrows. "It has that effect on people," she joked.

"Will you spend the day with me?" Diane's voice had grown more serious. "I still owe you dinner, after all."

"I'd love to, but I do need to get home to Bramble. She'll be going bonkers by now."

"I'll go with you." Diane put a hand on Tamsin's knee. "If you want me to, of course."

"We might as well tell Bramble," Tamsin said. "She's the least judgmental creature I know."

———

On the walk from Diane's home to Tamsin's cottage, Tamsin had wanted to take Diane's hand in hers, but she'd fought the urge. After all, she wasn't the one who'd lived in this village all her life. She figured that, for Diane, just being seen walking through Tynebury with the new lesbian in town was enough of a challenge already. But if it was, Diane hadn't let on at all. Despite their hands not touching, Tamsin had felt close to her because Diane had barely seemed to notice any passers-by— she'd only had eyes for Tamsin.

After lavishing Bramble with enough attention to make up for having to spend the night on her own—a few extra treats and throwing her tennis ball into the thicket of shrubs bordering the property—they stood in Tamsin's kitchen.

"Do you, er, want to talk about what happened?" Tamsin asked.

Diane pursed her lips and locked her gaze on Tamsin's. "I think I might have to do it all over again before I can talk about it."

Tamsin burst into a chuckle. "We do have all day so I suppose that can be arranged." She stepped closer and pushed herself against Diane, pressing her backside against the kitchen counter. They kissed and any desire to talk fled Tamsin as well.

When they broke from their kiss, Diane said, "I don't want to think about any of the consequences of this. Not yet. I just want to enjoy it." She ran a fingertip over Tamsin's upper arm.

"Excellent plan." Diane probably didn't realise that this was a departure from Tamsin's usual ways as well. But it felt good—different. Full of possibility. And they may not be at the exact same stage of their lives, but they already had a lot more in common than Tamsin and Ellen had ever had. In fact, Ellen hadn't crossed Tamsin's mind much at all in the past twenty-four hours. This was a first.

They'd just locked lips again when Tamsin's phone started ringing. She rolled her eyes. "I bet you that's my loving, but very nosy sister." She dug her phone out of her purse and showed Diane the screen, which displayed a picture of Eve pulling a silly face. If it had been anyone else, Tamsin would have pressed the ignore button already, but she'd always had a hard time ignoring Eve. It wasn't something they did with each other. Although this time, Eve couldn't possibly use the excuse she'd worry if Tamsin didn't pick up. They both knew why she was calling.

"Are you going to pick up?" Diane asked.

Tamsin had only to look at Diane, her head tilted back, her eyes full of desire, to be able to ignore her twin. "Eve can wait," she said, and tapped the red button. She switched her phone to silent mode and tossed it back into her bag.

"What if there's a golfing emergency at the club today?" Diane said, a wide smirk on her face. "What if Debbie gets a ball stuck in the bunker again and needs to reach you urgently because she has no clue how to get it out?"

"Really?" Tamsin stepped closer again. "Debbie's who you're thinking of right now?"

"Screw Debbie." Diane hooked a finger in the waist of Tamsin's jeans and pulled her all the way to her. "I feel kind of sorry for her now, actually. She's stuck with Lawrence while I've got you."

———

"My dad made this very bed we're lying in," Tamsin said. They had to stop ending up in bed around meal times because her stomach was growling again.

"It's very sturdy." Diane turned to her side. Tamsin adored her playful side. "Give him my compliments." She kissed Tamsin on the nose. "What about the bedside tables? They're gorgeous."

Pride swelled in Tamsin's chest. "I bought those for ten quid each at a charity shop in London, then gave them a new life."

"A charity shop?" Diane sat up a bit straighter. "They look like they come from a designer store."

Tamsin held up her hand and wiggled her fingers. "The magic Foxley touch."

"I know all about that." Diane caught Tamsin's hand in hers and kissed the tip of her index finger. "It must be magic, what with you managing to get me into bed twice in less than twenty-four hours."

Tamsin cleared her throat ostentatiously. "Excuse me. I thought I was coming over to yours for dinner last night, only to find out that no dinner would be served. At all. This is not my doing at all."

"You're too foxy, Tamsin Foxley," Diane said and snickered. "I bet you've heard that one a million times before."

"A few times, but it sounds extra adorable coming from you." Tamsin slanted towards Diane and pulled her into a kiss again. She couldn't get enough of her.

A phone started ringing downstairs. They both jumped.

"That can't be me. I've put mine on silent," Tamsin said, while making a mental note to call Eve at the earliest opportunity.

"Must be mine then." Diane sighed. "Do you mind if I get that? What with Lucy being pregnant. It could be Timothy."

"Of course." Tamsin watched Diane get out of bed—a sight she'd missed that morning—and quickly slip into her blouse.

"There's a robe on the back of the door," Tamsin said.

Diane nodded and grabbed it, then headed downstairs. Tamsin followed her with a sheet folded around her naked body. Diane had missed the call, but it was apparently from someone important enough—probably her son—for her to call back immediately.

CHAPTER TWENTY-THREE

"Mum," Tim answered after only one ring. "Where are you? We're at the house, but you're not here."

"You're at my house?" Panic surged inside Diane. "What are you doing there? Did we have plans?"

Diane looked towards Tamsin. The sight of her wrapped only in a sheet drew Diane's attention away from Timothy's voice in her ear. The only thing Diane wanted right then was to drop the phone, unwrap Tamsin and do things to her she had never deemed possible before last night.

"Mum?" Timothy's voice came louder now. "Are you there?"

"Sorry, darling," Diane tried to drag her mind back to the call. "I lost you there for a second. What were you saying?"

"We're on our way to a baby furniture sale near Eastbourne and figured we'd stop by to say hi."

"Of course, I'm just out for a walk," Diane lied. "I'll be home in about fifteen minutes." She hung up and looked down at herself. First things first, she needed her clothes. She went to stand in front of Tamsin.

"Do you have to leave?" Tamsin grabbed hold of her hand and pulled her close to her.

"Tim and Lucy have dropped by out of the blue." Diane put her head on Tamsin's shoulder.

"Then you should go meet them," Tamsin said softly. "Even though I'm quite reluctant to let you out of here." She kissed Diane's head.

"I know," Diane said on a sigh. "I don't want to leave." She extricated herself from Tamsin's embrace. "They're on their way somewhere, so they won't stay too long. I'll come back here as soon as I can get rid of them?" Diane couldn't believe she was talking about her son and daughter-in-law like that.

"Take your time, I'm not going anywhere." Tamsin kissed her softly on the lips and Diane rushed upstairs to make herself presentable.

———

Diane entered her home to find Timothy and Lucy in the living room, looking at something on an iPad. They stood when they saw her and Timothy came around the coffee table to come give his mother a kiss.

"Hello darling," Diane said. Lucy had joined them and Diane embraced her. "How are you both? How's the baby?"

As she was walking over from Tamsin's cottage Diane had done her best to assume a calm and normal demeanour. She did not want to spark any suspicion of anything unusual in Timothy.

"We're both doing great," Lucy said, rubbing her hand over her belly. "I had a check-up on Thursday and everything is as it should be."

"I'm more curious about how you're doing, Mum," Tim said, adopting a stern look. "I couldn't help but notice the two empty wine glasses on the table here."

Diane looked down at the table. In the excitement of what had happened last night, and the rush to get back to Bramble, she'd forgotten to tidy up the remnants of the evening. She looked back up at Timothy and saw the teasing look in his eyes.

"Did you have a visit from a suitor last night?" he asked.

Panic gripped Diane and she tried to keep her face as straight as she could. "Don't be ridiculous, dear. It was just Isabelle. We had a drink, but I was too tired to clean up. If I'd known you were coming, I would have made the house spic and span." She gave him what she hoped was an ironic smile. "Now, who would like a cup of tea?"

She walked towards the kitchen, hoping they wouldn't follow so she'd have time to get rid of the evidence that someone had been there for breakfast.

The previous night had been amazing and exciting and like nothing she could have imagined, but it had also overwhelmed her. She was definitely not ready to talk about it with Timothy yet. Not that she expected he would react badly to the idea of his mother seeing another woman. He was a child of his time, after all, and she had never heard him utter a single negative comment about Rob or any other gay person he had encountered. It was Diane herself who needed to wrap her head around it, who needed to process what had unfolded between her and Tamsin.

"Is everything all right, Mum?"

Diane jumped. She hadn't heard Timothy walk into the kitchen as she was gathering cups and saucers for their tea.

"Yes, darling, of course it is," Diane said, sending Tim her most motherly smile.

"You just seem a bit..." He paused and tilted his head, as if examining a patient. "There's something about you today. I can't quite put my finger on it. Are you sure there's nothing you need to tell me?"

Diane picked up the tray on which she had placed the crockery and handed it to her son. "I don't know what you're on about. Here, take that into the living room."

She picked up her handbag and took out her compact. In her rush to get back home from Tamsin's she hadn't really looked at herself, other than to pull a comb through her hair. It was hard to say peering into the small mirror, but maybe she did look a little different. Her features seemed more relaxed, and she was smiling exuberantly. She tried to adopt a more serious expression, but every time the edges of her mouth seemed to inch up of their own volition. It probably had to do with the fact that images kept floating to the forefront of her mind. Tamsin as she pulled her in to kiss her; as she let her eyes roam over Diane's body after undressing her; as she dipped her head beneath the sheets to—Diane gave her head a small shake to dismiss that image.

She looked into the mirror again. A slight blush had crept into her cheeks now. She hoped Timothy would not comment on it.

The kettle started whistling and she took it off the stove. She poured water into the teapot and took it into the living room.

———

Timothy and Lucy had not lingered at Diane's after having a cup of tea, as they had to carry on to Eastbourne. The sale was all recycled stuff and they wanted to be as environmentally-friendly as possible and not buy all new stuff for the baby.

All the talk of vintage furniture had brought Tamsin to Diane's mind even more than she was already. Maybe Diane could ask her to restore something that she could give Tim and Lucy for the baby's room.

Diane was impatient to get back to Tamsin. It was still early in the afternoon and they would be able to spend quite a few hours together. At the same time she felt she should take this time she had away from Tamsin to consider what had happened. She knew that as soon as she went back to Tamsin's she would be unable to keep herself from enjoying the newly rediscovered physical pleasures.

Of course, every time she thought about last night, and this morning, her desire to return to Tamsin kept getting bigger and more unavoidable.

She decided she needed to speak to someone neutral, to rationalise things. She picked up her phone and called Isabelle.

"Please tell me you have some juicy details," Isabelle greeted her. So much for polite hellos.

"I'm very well, thank you Isabelle. How are you?" Diane decided she wasn't going to give in to her friend's request so easily.

"Come on, don't keep me waiting," Isabelle insisted. "How did the date go? What did you cook? Did you do some more smooching?"

Diane tried to think of diplomatic ways to tell Isabelle about the previous night, but came up short. "It went well. We had toast and Marmite. And yes, we did kiss some more. Any other questions?"

"Oh, oh, slow down." Diane could hear the agitation in Isabelle's voice. "Toast and Marmite? What kind of a dinner is that?" She went quiet for a second. Then Diane heard a gasp on the other end of the line. "Did you only manage to serve toast because you were too busy serving *yourself* up to her—so to speak?"

Diane giggled. "Maybe," she said coyly.

Another gasp. "Diane Thompson, you sly minx, I can't believe it. So how was it? I know I said I wanted the juicy details, but now that there actually *are* juicy details, I think broad strokes will do."

Diane sighed. "It was unbelievable. She's—she's just unbelievable. I never knew it could be like this. I know I don't have masses of experience to compare it with. I've only ever slept with three men—that includes Lawrence. But, Isabelle, it's like she touched something deep inside me."

Isabelle chuckled. "Quite literally, I would think."

Diane pretended not to hear her friend's comment and continued. "I feel like my life has been changed fundamentally and now I don't know how to get on with it."

"You're in love," Isabelle said, her voice gentle now. "You probably don't remember what it's like, but that's what it is."

Diane thought about this. Could she really be in love with Tamsin? So quickly and unexpectedly? She tried to recall the early days of her and Lawrence's courtship. They had been in love, that was for sure, and passionate, at least in the first few years. But this felt so much bigger, so much more life-altering.

"I suppose you're right." Diane threw her head back. "But right now I feel more like a randy teenager. All I can think about is getting back to her place so we can go another round."

"Do you mean she's waiting for you right now?" Isabelle sounded aghast. "Then what are you doing on the phone with me. Go, be with her. Call me tomorrow. We can talk about it some more. From what I gather, you lesbians love to process."

It was Diane's turn to gasp, but Isabelle had already hung up before she could utter a word of protest.

———

Twenty minutes later, Diane arrived at Tamsin's cottage. As she opened the gate, Bramble came bounding towards her, greeting her with a lick on the hand.

Diane walked around the house to the garden and found Tamsin in a lounger, fast asleep. Her head was turned slightly to the side and her hands were held together on her belly. Diane didn't want to disturb the peaceful tableau in front of her.

She crept over to the chair next to Tamsin and sat,

stretching her legs in front of her. The chair gave a small squeak.

Tamsin turned towards her and opened her eyes. She gave Diane a languorous smile. "I nodded off. I think you drained me of all my energy."

Diane smiled back at her. "Aren't you fourteen years younger than me? Shouldn't I be the one exhausted by last night's shenanigans?"

Tamsin gave a small laugh. "Is that what we're calling it? Because seeing you is giving me back my strength. I think I might be up to some more shenanigans pretty soon."

"I sure hope so." Diane stretched out her arm and placed her hand on Tamsin's. "This old lady seems to have discovered a new source of energy and can't wait to tap into it once more."

"If you put it like that," Tamsin said. She stood and swung one leg over Diane, straddling her. She took Diane's face in her hands and gave her a slow, sensual kiss. "We mustn't let your levels dip." She kissed her again, moving her hands down Diane's body.

Diane could feel her body heating up at Tamsin's touch. "Let's go inside," she said.

CHAPTER TWENTY-FOUR

Tamsin stretched her arms above her head. The sheet slipped down and she found herself staring at her own naked breasts. Tamsin had never been able to sleep fully in the nude—it just wasn't her thing—yet here she lay, in the buff. She turned her head to look at the cause of her nudity in bed. Diane was still sleeping. She lay on her side facing away from Tamsin.

They'd spent two nights in a row together, so this definitely was no longer a one-night stand. Not that Tamsin had ever considered it that, but Diane might have. She might not have come back to Tamsin's house last night. After she'd left to meet her son, Tamsin hadn't been able to keep that thought from popping into her head. What was going through Diane's mind as she'd left? As she spoke to her son? At least Tamsin had always been sure of one thing in her adult life: her attraction to women. She had no idea how it felt to come across this particular attraction in your fifties, after living a life of heterosexuality.

Tamsin tried to imagine falling for a man in approximately fifteen years, but the thought was simply too far-fetched—and the prospect too far in the future. This wasn't something you imagined beforehand, she figured. It was something that happened to you.

Diane had been all over her last night, much bolder in her actions than the night before already, and her enthusiasm hadn't left much room for doubt in Tamsin's mind. She had admired Tamsin's body, had called it youthful and delicious— ironically, two words Tamsin had often stamped on her own younger lovers. She was the younger lover now, but also the more experienced one. The whole thing was a wonderful new adventure altogether.

She looked at her alarm clock. It would start playing Radio Four in one minute. The weekend was over. They both had to get back into the real world, pick up their regular lives and engage in far more ordinary activities than the extremely pleasant ones they'd occupied themselves with over the weekend.

Tamsin rolled over, as though she wanted to protect Diane from the upcoming noise of radio presenters on a Monday morning. She slung an arm over Diane's middle and pressed her body against Diane's warm back. The simple pleasure of waking up beside another woman engulfed her and she inhaled Diane's scent. Then the alarm started blaring and Diane stirred. She let out a little groan and pressed herself into Tamsin's embrace.

"Good god," she said, after a few seconds. "Will you please turn off that monstrous racket?"

"What are you on about? This is Radio Four. Isn't that what golfing accountants in Tynebury listen to?"

"Not at this ungodly hour of the morning." Diane croaked, bringing an inadvertent smile to Tamsin's lips.

"It's seven o'clock. I'd hardly call that ungodly. It's light outside already."

Diane grabbed hold of Tamsin's arm and nestled herself

deeper into her spooning hug. "It *is* when I'm in bed with you and all I want to do is stay here for as long as possible."

"Well, here's an idea." Tamsin planted a quick kiss on the back of her head. "Come back tonight."

"You've got great ideas for a Monday morning." Diane kissed Tamsin on the lower arm, then started turning over in her arms. She swivelled her body around until she lay facing Tamsin. "Good morning, by the way." Her sleepy face melted into a smile.

"Morning, gorgeous," Tamsin said, and went in for a kiss, starting to wonder how they would ever get out of this bed.

"I wish it were May already, then we'd have a couple of bank holiday Mondays," Diane said. "We timed this wrong." She shook her head. "We should have had our first date on the eve of a long weekend."

"Our first sex date, you mean."

Diane chuckled. "We should take a week off, really." She ran her hand over Tamsin's belly. "Or a few. I want to take my time getting to know this heavenly body."

"How about lunch," Tamsin said. "I'll be at the club all day."

Diane's hand stiffened against her stomach.

Tamsin could kick herself. Too much, too soon. She'd been too caught up in the moment. Too intoxicated by waking up next to Diane.

"Forget I said that." She sent Diane a reassuring smile. "Let's just meet up this evening."

"I'd love to have lunch with you." Diane's body seemed to loosen a little. "But maybe not at the club. Not yet."

"It's fine, Diane." Tamsin stroked her thumb over Diane's shoulder. "Let's just take it easy. The words were out of my mouth before I even realised."

Diane rolled onto her back. "While my body seems to be adjusting at a very rapid speed, my brain may need a little time to catch up."

"Hey." Tamsin scooted closer and put her hand on Diane's belly. "We have all the time in the world." During the short silence that fell, the radio presenter announced that it was seven minutes past seven. "Except for maybe right now," Tamsin said. She had a meeting with the club secretary at half past eight. When they'd set the meeting, that time hadn't seemed odd to her at all because they'd both proclaimed themselves early birds—and Tamsin liked to keep the bulk of her day free of meetings so she had more time to teach. Now, she cursed the early arrangement.

"I need to get going as well. Tax season isn't over yet." Diane didn't brush Tamsin's hand away, nor did she make any movement to slide from underneath the covers.

"It's going to be all right," Tamsin said, because she felt she needed to say something.

"My brain will do just fine catching up." Diane smiled up at her. "Meanwhile, I'll just let my body take the lead."

———

It felt different to arrive at the club after the weekend Tamsin had just had. She had a spring in her step and while she thought the secretary a bit dull—Dennis took his tasks so seriously, there didn't seem to be any room for even the tiniest bit of banter—she didn't mind sitting across from him, listening to him drone on about all things RTGB related.

By the time Tamsin had taught her second lesson of the day, and she was in the locker room taking off her golf shoes before going to the restaurant for lunch, it started to seriously dawn on her that she might be falling in love. Images of a smiling Diane kept popping up in her mind, alternating with images of Diane in ecstasy—that most private facial expression to share with another person—and images of Diane utterly relaxed in her embrace. Tamsin couldn't wait for tonight, and the night after, and all the ones after that. Although, again, she seemed to be getting slightly ahead of herself.

She walked into the restaurant and ordered her usual salad from Linda behind the counter. She sat at her regular table overlooking the course in all its glory—a sight she'd never get bored of, especially in springtime when everything was bursting back into life. She compared it to how she felt—the flowers of love blossoming boldly in her heart.

Tamsin was pulled from her reverie by two women entering the restaurant. Isabelle and Barbara. In Portugal, she had learned they were both true ladies of leisure. Isabelle's husband still, very old-fashioned in Tamsin's opinion, brought home the bacon—it was how Isabelle had put it herself. Tamsin couldn't help but wonder who brought home the proverbial bacon in Barbara's household of one. Or did she have a secret sugar mummy? She chuckled at the thought.

Isabelle waved at her and walked over. "How lovely to see you," she said, in a manner so enthusiastic Tamsin had no choice but to believe her. "Did you have a nice weekend?" She cocked her head.

"Lovely, and you?" Tamsin replied.

"Fine." Isabelle narrowed her eyes. "What did you do that might've been so lovely?"

"Just this and that." Tamsin thought about saying 'working on some old furniture' but if Diane had confided in her friend already, which Tamsin believed she might very well have done, what with the way Isabelle was scrutinising her, it might come across as a little disrespectful. "Taking Bramble for long walks and such."

"I see." Isabelle tapped a finger against her chin, as though she was about to figure out the final piece of a very complex puzzle.

"Sorry we can't join you," Barbara said. "We're supposed to

welcome one of the new members today. Have lunch with her, make her feel at home."

"Thank goodness it's not Debbie." Isabelle rolled her eyes. "She seems to feel welcome enough already."

This earned her a jab in the elbow from Barbara.

"Yes, yes, I know. But that woman stole my best friend's husband and still has the nerve to prance about the place as though she actually belongs here and all the while Rob—"

"Yes, yes," Barbara said, matter-of-factly. "If they apply again next year, we'll make sure Rob gets accepted. No excuses. Times are changing around here." She let her gaze linger on Tamsin for a beat.

"We'll have to see about that." Isabelle sighed.

Linda approached with Tamsin's salad.

"Enjoy your lunch," Isabelle said, locking eyes with Tamsin a little longer than Tamsin would normally expect. What was up with these ladies today? Was it the arrival of spring in the air? Or was it something about Tamsin's face that gave away what she'd really been up to over the weekend?

After thanking Linda, Tamsin put a hand to her cheek, to feel for marks that might have been left after an unexpectedly hot weekend with one of this club's members. All she felt were her lips drawn into a perpetual smile.

She got out her phone and sent Diane a message. She didn't say anything about Isabelle's quizzing or Barbara's lingering look. Instead, she typed: *How many hours until I see you again?*

Tamsin scoffed at her own lameness. This wasn't the sort of text you sent to a sophisticated woman like Diane Thompson. It was most definitely the sort of exchanges she and Ellen had engaged in, endlessly and, Tamsin had to admit, at times nauseatingly. Diane might be the one standing on the brink of her first same-sex relationship but Tamsin was very much there with her, ready to embark on her first truly adult one.

CHAPTER TWENTY-FIVE

"Hold your hands a little higher when you're addressing the ball," Tamsin said, lifting Diane's hands and the club they were gripping by an inch. "This is a seven iron, not a driver."

Diane felt her posture straighten slightly as a consequence. She was trying to keep her focus on hitting the ball nice and straight, but Tamsin's touch, innocuous as it was, made it very hard. She swung her club back, paused for a fraction of a second at the top, and then brought the club back towards the ball. The ball flew straight to the right side of the driving range, not rising more than three feet above the ground.

Diane looked at Tamsin sheepishly. "I guess I have to adjust to this new position of my hands."

Tamsin chuckled. "You need to keep your eyes on the ball for longer when you hit. No need to look up so soon, I'll see where it goes."

"I suppose I'm finding it hard to keep my eyes focused on anything else than you these days." Diane gave Tamsin a goofy grin.

It had been ten days since their first night together. In that time they had seen each other almost every evening and woken up together almost every morning. They had taken the car down to the seaside at the weekend, had walked along the beach, and had arrived back in Tynebury in the evening exhausted, but even more hungry for each other than before. The seaside air acting as a potent aphrodisiac.

When they weren't exploring the physical pleasures of a blossoming new relationship, Diane and Tamsin spent most of the time talking, about everything. They had discussed their childhood, places they'd travelled to, the National Health Service. They had opened up about their ambitions for themselves when they were young and how they felt they'd fulfilled them.

In Tamsin's presence Diane felt like a giddy hormonal teenager who wanted more and more of that sensual intimacy she had only just discovered. At the same time, their affair felt so mature and full of the companionship everyone aspired to have with a person they wanted to share the rest of their life with. Because when Diane pictured her future now, Tamsin was an inextricable part of it.

When they were apart during the day Diane found herself checking the clock constantly, counting the hours and minutes until she could leave the office and join Tamsin at her cottage or go home and wait for Tamsin to arrive.

They'd been living in a bubble ever since that first night. They had only spent time together inside their homes or away from Tynebury and the golf club. Tamsin had asked Diane a couple of times to join her for lunch at the club or to meet her in the village for a drink after work, but Diane had found an excuse to say no every time.

When they had woken that morning, Tamsin had reminded Diane that she had booked a lesson with her a couple of weeks ago, before they had grown closer to each other. Diane's first thought had been to cancel. She did not feel ready to be seen in public with Tamsin, even if what they would be doing was completely innocent. But as Diane had opened her mouth to tell Tamsin she wanted to cancel the lesson, she'd found Tamsin looking at her with such expectation, she couldn't bring herself to say the words out loud. And anyway, their lesson was planned for nine-thirty on a Wednesday. There would hardly be anyone at the club to witness the two of them together.

Tamsin placed a new ball in front of Diane. "Really focus on keeping your head down as long as possible this time. Don't worry about where the ball goes."

Diane set herself up, hands higher than what felt comfortable. She swung and kept her eyes on the ball until the momentum of her arms and body made her head turn towards the range. She saw the ball she'd just hit fly high and straight towards the distance marker she had been aiming for.

"Excellent," Tamsin said encouragingly. "That kind of shot deserves a kiss." Tamsin took a step closer to Diane, but must have seen the look of panic on her face. She moved back to her previous position, sadness on her face.

"I'm sorry," Diane said quickly. "I know it's ridiculous to be so paranoid about someone seeing us. I don't want you to feel I'm ashamed or anything like that." She held out her hand and placed it on Tamsin's arm in what she hoped was a reassuring gesture.

"It's all right." Tamsin smiled at her, but Diane could see a trace of trepidation in her eyes. "I got ahead of myself a bit again. I'll try to keep myself under better control when we're in public." Now a more mischievous grin appeared on her face. "As long as I can give you your deserved reward tonight."

"I most certainly hope you will," Diane said, desire bubbling up inside of her at the thought of what Tamsin might have in store for her.

————

Diane towelled herself off carefully. Her lesson with Tamsin had only taken thirty minutes, but it was exceptionally warm today and she'd worked up a bit of a sweat. Not to mention the increase in body temperature that always occurred just from being in Tamsin's vicinity. She had definitely needed a shower before heading to the office.

She heard the door to the changing room open.

"… And she told me I should think of investing in a new rescue wood," a woman's voice said as she walked in. Diane didn't recognise it.

"I got mine from Greensome's. You should go have a look." Diane did recognise the second voice. Debbie.

Diane stood still in the shower stall, hoping the two women were only there to change shoes and would be out again quickly.

"Have you tried out the new teacher yet?" Debbie asked her friend.

"Not yet. How is she?"

"She's great," Debbie replied enthusiastically. At least Diane agreed with her on that. "I feel like I'm improving a little every time I have a session with her. I love that they hired someone not too old to replace Darren. And a woman."

"Everyone seems quite smitten with her," the unidentified woman said. She must be one of the new members whom Diane hadn't met yet. "And clearly not just the men. Do you have a bit of a crush on her, Deborah?"

"A bit of a girl crush, maybe."

Oh god, Diane thought. First Debbie had stolen her husband, now she had a crush on Diane's lover?

Lover. Was that what Tamsin was? She could hardly call her her girlfriend. Surely women in their fifties did not have girl-friends.

"She does have that whole sporty, slightly androgynous thing going on," Debbie continued. Her voice was coming from much closer to Diane's shower stall now. "I can definitely understand the appeal, if one was that way inclined." She giggled

Diane heard a tap being switched on and hands being washed.

"Well," the other woman said in a conspiratorial tone. She also sounded as if she was standing much closer to Diane than she had been before. "Speaking of Tamsin's appeal. I heard something just yesterday that you may find rather interesting."

Diane held her breath to keep perfectly quiet. She did not want to miss anything of the conversation if the topic was Tamsin.

"You know Morag, who works at the Co-op? She told me that she was on her way to work on Monday morning—this was dead early; seven o'clock or something—and she saw Tamsin leave a house that wasn't hers." The woman paused to take a breath. "At that time of day, it could only be a walk of shame, don't you think?"

"I suppose so," Diane heard Debbie say. "Do you know whose house it was?"

"That's the best bit." The woman's voice lowered now, as if she was worried someone would overhear them, but Diane could still hear her very clearly. "She said it was your Lawrence's old house."

Diane's mouth fell open.

She heard a gasp on the other side of the shower door. Then Debbie said, "You're joking."

"I'm not. I asked Morag twice to be sure. Do you think it's possible? Could there be something going on between Tamsin and Lawrence's ex?"

Diane's legs turned to jelly and she pressed her hand against the wall to steady herself. They had been so discreet. But still someone was on to them. She loved her village life in Tynebury, but right at that moment she wished for the anonymity of a big city.

Debbie took her time to reply. "Lawrence did mention once that he had a suspicion Diane might swing both ways. Not that she had ever done anything, I think. I just assumed it was some kind of wishful thinking on his part. To make her more interesting and justify why he stayed with her for so long." She paused. "I just can't believe someone as stuck up and boring could do something so..."

"Exciting?" The woman completed Debbie's sentence. "Maybe she's not as boring and stuck up as you think she is."

Diane's mortification was turning into anger now. She was of half a mind to walk out from the stall and confirm the rumour, just to prove to Debbie how wrong her image of Diane was.

But of course, she didn't.

"Maybe not," Debbie said with a giggle. "I can't wait to tell Lawrence."

The two women had finished washing their hands and, Diane guessed, were walking towards the door, as their voices started to grow more distant.

Diane felt like she had been holding her breath forever and exhaled as she heard the door to the changing room slam shut. Everything was quiet again, except for Diane's heartbeat reverberating in her ears.

If Debbie knew there was something going on between her and Tamsin, then soon the whole club would know. Unless she and Tamsin came up with a plausible explanation for what she had been doing at Diane's so early in the morning.

She hoped Debbie's path wouldn't cross Tamsin's before Diane had a chance to talk to her so they could get their stories straight.

Diane waited for another minute before stepping out of the

stall. She got dressed much more quickly than she had planned, not bothering to put on her make up. She'd fix her face at the office.

Once she was ready she exited the changing room and headed for the clubhouse doors. There, she paused and stared at the path to the car park, scanning her surroundings for any sign of Debbie. The coast seemed clear, so she hurried to her car and drove to the office. She had a feeling it would not be the most productive of days.

CHAPTER TWENTY-SIX

Tamsin shook her head and a hundred rain drops fell to the floor. She'd been caught in a downpour with Bramble and her next urgent task was to dry off the dog before she tracked mud throughout the cottage. She was busy performing that arduous task when she heard a car door slam. Her heart leapt. Diane.

She gave Bramble's paws a quick inspection and patted the dog on the head. "That'll have to do, girl. My lady has arrived." Her lips curved into a smile as she rushed to the front door to let Diane in—Bramble hot on her heels.

Diane looked scrumptious as ever, better even, according to Tamsin, because she'd gone light on the makeup, and her hair was a little less sculpted than usual.

Tamsin waited until Diane was safely inside before drawing her into a hug. Diane stood stiffly in her embrace.

"What's going on?" Tamsin took a step back, but left her hands on Diane's shoulders.

"It's out. Debbie knows about us which means by now the entire village must know." She took a deep breath but it didn't seem to calm her down much.

"Okay." Tamsin took her by the hand and led her inside the living room. Bramble tried to get Diane to pet her, but she wasn't getting much attention. "Let's sit so you can tell me all about it."

Diane looked into Tamsin's eyes for only a fleeting second before her glance skittered away. She didn't once look at Tamsin as she spoke. "Someone saw you leave my house early in the morning. Word is spreading quickly. I overheard Debbie, of all people, talking about me." She shook her head. "I can just imagine the conversation she's having with Lawrence right about now." She looked at her watch. "He's probably just come home from work. She's probably prepared him a drink, her cheeks hurting from the smile she hasn't been able to wipe off her face since she heard the news."

"Diane." Tamsin thought it better to keep her distance. "It's all right."

"Is it?" She pushed air through her nostrils. "It's easy enough for you to say. I've lived here my entire life. I've had to go through the humiliation of the most cliché divorce you can imagine, but I always held my head up high, even on the days when it was bloody hard. But to have people talking behind my back again about... About—" She stopped abruptly.

"About us," Tamsin said.

"About something..." The volume of Diane's voice had lowered. "...so very private and"—she threw up her hands —"something even I, frankly, haven't been able to wrap my head around entirely. What chance do we even stand if we have to face people's scrutiny and gossip every day?" Her hands landed in her lap. "This is just not how I wanted things to go. I don't know what to do."

"Hey." Tamsin did scoot a little closer now. "I understand you're upset."

"You were talking about latebians the other day." Diane's voice had grown in force again. "If there's a latebian manual, I'd very much like to have that at my disposal right now. How do they do it? Face people they've known all their lives and tell them, or no, not just tell them, but stand up to them and—"

"Diane." Tamsin reached for one of Diane's hands. "Look at me, please." Tamsin curved her lips into the most comforting smile she could muster.

Diane finally looked at her again. She wasn't crying, but, behind her glasses, her eyes were red. Her cheeks were flushed —and not in the good way Tamsin had come to know.

"It's a shock to have to hear things like that being said about you, but in the grand scheme of things, it doesn't mean that much." Tamsin stroked her thumb over Diane's palm. "What matters is what we have between us. People will always talk."

"But it's taking away from what we have between us."

"How so?" Tamsin asked.

"How can it be like it was before, now that everyone's talking about us?"

"Because..." Tamsin needed to take a deep breath herself. "Inside this house, behind that door you just closed, nothing has changed. We're still the same. We're still falling in love." She narrowed her eyes. "I'm still massively besotted with you."

Diane withdrew her hand from Tamsin's grasp. "It's different for you. You've been a lesbian all your life. I—I have a son. I'm going to be a grandmother, for heaven's sake." She took off her glasses. Tamsin always thought she looked so much more vulnerable without them—as though they were her armour against the outside world which could be so cruel. "I need to talk to Lawrence." She pushed herself out of the sofa.

"Diane." Tamsin used her stern teacher voice. "You're spinning out of control."

Bramble let out a small bark at the raising of voices.

"Tell me what to do to make this stop." Diane clutched her hand to her chest. "This feeling inside. It's like all the good memories I've accumulated over the past ten days are being torn to shreds by dread, by this fear I don't know how to deal with."

"What you feel is completely normal." Tamsin tried to find Diane's gaze again but it proved a challenge. She rose and stood in front of her. "Please know that you're not alone in this. I'm here with you."

Diane pinched the bridge of her nose. "I'm not entirely sure I can do this."

"Do what?" The dread Diane was just talking about seemed to have found its way inside Tamsin as well.

"*This*. Be with you. Be with another woman. It must have been some form of temporary insanity."

"Do you really care that much about what people in the village say about you?"

"It's not just that... most of my clients are local."

"What do your clients have to do with anything?" Tamsin couldn't help a hint of anger slipping into her voice. This was starting to remind her of when she got fired at her previous club. Let's get rid of the lesbian pro and pretend nothing ever happened—as though such a thing were even possible.

"You don't understand. I'm not like you, Tamsin. I'm not a... lesbian."

Tamsin put her hands on her hips. "You very much were in bed with me last night. And there is such a thing as bisexual, you know."

Diane shook her head and repositioned her glasses. She blew out a lungful of air. "I just don't want to be judged on something that I'm not even sure of yet."

Tamsin took a step back and buried her hands in the pockets of her jeans. "People talk. They've always done so and they always will," she managed to say. "You do it; I do it. It's hard at first, until they find something else to talk about and everyone moves on." Tamsin was grateful for Bramble who'd come to stand next to her. She crouched next to her dog.

"I've been through this once before when Lawrence left me. You've no idea how much energy it took me to put that behind me."

"What is it you're trying to tell me?" Tamsin hugged Bramble. She wasn't sure she wanted to hear what Diane was going to say next. But she sure as hell wasn't going to stand for this nonsense.

"I think I may need some time to figure out what I really want."

"Oh, you mean to find out what's most important to you: how we feel about each other or what people who have nothing to do with it have to say about it." Tamsin pushed herself up to her full length. "I stopped defending who I am a long time ago, Diane." The sight of Diane looking so torn melted something in her nonetheless. "If only you knew how many women—and men, for that matter—have been in your exact position before. This is a tale as old as time. Just like Lawrence leaving you for Debbie. I'm sure he had to endure his fair share of gossip, not in the least from you and your friends at the club."

"He cheated on me," Diane snarled. "It was no less than he deserved and you can't possibly compare the two."

Tamsin held out her hands, but they fell idly in the space—the increasing distance—between them. "Don't go. Please."

In the silence that followed, and even though the cottage was set back from the street, they could hear footsteps. Bramble was the first to look up and press her snout against the window. The cottage was on the edge of town and it was rare for people to walk past, especially in this weather.

Both Tamsin and Diane glanced out of the window. Two figures underneath a bright pink umbrella stood at the edge of the driveway.

Diane slanted towards the window. "I'm sure that's Debbie. She must be spying on me."

Tamsin couldn't suppress a chuckle. It was as much the

release of tension she so desperately needed, as well as the antics of the village residents that genuinely made her laugh.

"It's not funny," Diane whispered. "My car's right in front of your door."

"So what if it's her? Then she has confirmation." Tamsin shrugged. "We should go outside right now and tell her she can stop speculating."

"Have you lost your mind?" Diane moved away from the window.

"I haven't, but it seems to me you have." Diane no longer looked like the ravishing woman Tamsin had ushered in mere minutes ago.

"I thought I could do this. I truly believed I could, just because you're so... utterly amazing." Diane's voice broke. "Please know that this has nothing to do with you, but I'm afraid I really can't do this. I can't be with you. This whole thing, it's just too much for me."

"Don't say something you'll regret later." Tamsin was torn between taking a step forward and throwing her arms around Diane and accepting that, perhaps, Diane was right and their short affair had already run its course. She might not have made the same old mistake of falling for someone much younger, but this wasn't turning out much better than her previous relationships. At least she could tick 'frightened straight woman' off her list now. Been there, done that. Much too complicated to ever try again.

"Of course I'll regret it." Diane's bottom lip quivered. "But if there's one thing I've learned in my fifty-four years, it's that regret is a fundamental part of life." She picked up her bag from the floor and slung it over her shoulder. "I'd better go."

"Diane." Tamsin did take that step forward now, spurred on by the acute fear spreading in her chest, but she was too late.

Before she disappeared into the hallway, Diane quickly turned around. "I'm sorry," was all she said.

CHAPTER TWENTY-SEVEN

Diane ran to her car and got in. The two people who had been staring at the cottage earlier were nowhere to be seen.

She looked around the car for something to dry herself off with. Rain was bucketing down and it had only taken the short distance from Tamsin's front door to Diane's car for her to get soaked. She found a small towel on the back seat and wiped her face with it.

She started the engine, doing her best not to glance back at the cottage. She didn't want to see Tamsin looking out of the window at her leaving. Or maybe she was afraid Tamsin wouldn't be staring after her at all. She drove off, not really thinking where she was going.

Tamsin's face crept to the forefront of her mind, and how it had gone from delight to incomprehension, to sorrow and finally anger, all in the space of a few minutes. All caused by Diane. A thick knot lodged itself in her gut.

She pulled the car to the side of the road. She shouldn't be driving around aimlessly in this dreadful weather.

The rational thing to do would be to just go back to

Tamsin's. Or maybe Isabelle's. Her friend would be sure to give her a pep talk. But Diane was feeling anything but rational and the one thought that kept pushing all others aside was that she needed to stop Debbie from telling everyone about her and Tamsin.

Of course, the very idea of having to confront Debbie was almost paralysing. But maybe she could talk to Lawrence. If she drove over now, and if one of the figures she'd seen lurking outside Tamsin's was indeed Debbie, she might beat her ex's new wife home. This was her chance to explain to Lawrence that Debbie had it all wrong and there was nothing going on between her and Tamsin. At least after her confrontation with Tamsin, it wouldn't be a lie. She pointed the car in the direction of Lawrence and Debbie's house.

They lived in a country house on the outskirts of Tynebury. Diane parked outside the gate. She peered towards the house, where she could see that lights were on.

Diane had driven past it many times, especially right after Lawrence their divorce, but she'd never been inside. She had a picture in her mind of a garish, over-the-top interior, with gilt and chrome fittings everywhere, more suited to a villa in Beverly Hills than a house in the English countryside. She'd know soon enough if reality matched her imagination.

I can't believe I'm doing this. Diane tried to realign her thoughts. Since the divorce she'd never had to consult Lawrence or rely on him for anything. Did she really think he was the right person to come to now? And was she really hoping he would forbid his wife to say something? More importantly: why did she care so much what other people might think?

Diane's hands were still gripping the steering wheel and she rested her head on them, trying to quieten the thoughts and questions swirling around in her mind. *You can still stop this ridiculousness and go back to Tamsin.* But again, the need to keep the whole thing quiet overrode every reasonable objection Diane could come up with.

She lifted her head and her hand moved to open the car door. It was as if her body had decided to take over now that her mind had been reduced to chaos. She stepped out of the car and walked up to the front door. The bell gave out an elaborate chime when she pressed it. A few seconds later the door opened and Lawrence stood in front of her.

"Diane," he said. "What are you doing here?" He looked genuinely surprised. Maybe Debbie hadn't told him anything yet.

"I need to talk to you. Can I come in?"

Lawrence moved aside to let her in.

Diane took in the entrance hall. The furniture was quite classic—a carved wooden cabinet, an elegant coat rack—but the decorative elements were very modern and very much what Diane had pictured to be Debbie's taste.

She handed her coat to Lawrence. "Is, er, Debbie home?"

"She's out with a friend tonight," Lawrence said. "I've only just arrived home myself." He led her into the living room and offered her a seat on the sofa. "Can I… get you a drink?" He looked unsure how to handle this impromptu visit.

Diane shook her head. "I won't be staying long. Have you spoken to Debbie at all today?"

Lawrence gave her a puzzled look. "Not since this morning. Why? What's going on? Did you get in a fight with her?" He gave a small chuckle, but she could see by the look on his face that he did not consider the suggestion completely impossible.

"Nothing like that," Diane said. "It's just…" Now she was here, she wasn't sure how to broach the subject she had come to discuss. How could she explain the situation without making herself look ridiculous for lurking in the shower stall and eavesdropping on Debbie's conversation? She decided she should just stick to a simplified version of the facts. Lawrence was a man after all, he would not be interested in the finer details.

"Today I overheard Debbie and a friend of hers—I don't know who—talking about me. They were saying things that could damage my reputation. Things that are just not true." She paused to take a breath.

Lawrence was still standing near the drinks cabinet, looking at her expectantly. When she didn't say anything for a few seconds, he sat in an armchair on the other side of the coffee table. "What things?" He spoke in a tone that was curious and gentle at the same time. He could probably see on Diane's face how much distress she was in.

"They said there was a rumour going around that I've been seeing someone. Having an affair if you will." She fell silent again. She cast her glance to her hands, which she was wringing together in her lap.

"Who are you rumoured to be having said affair with?"

The knot in her stomach moved up, as if it was trying to cut off her power of speech. But she had to say it, that was the whole point of her presence here. She had to address the rumour so it could go away. "With Tamsin, the new pro at the club."

"I see," Lawrence said calmly. He did not sound nearly as surprised as Diane had expected.

Diane looked up to meet his gaze. "It's not true." She tried to keep her voice steady, but she could hear a tremor in it. Her eyes were starting to well up so she looked back down at her hands again, willing the impending tears to retreat.

She heard Lawrence get up and take a few steps. Next, the sound of ice being dropped in a glass and some liquid being poured. She looked up as he came to sit next to her on the sofa and handed her a tumbler with what smelled like scotch in it.

"I think you may need this." He gave her a gentle smile. "Diane, clearly this is about more than a silly rumour. I've never known you to care much about what people say about you behind your back. Especially if what they're saying is false. Which leads me to believe that this so called rumour might not be false at all."

This was the trigger for Diane's tears to burst loose. She gave a couple of hiccupy sobs. Her nose was starting to run. Oh, how she hated the whole process of crying. Even when Lawrence had sat her down to announce he was leaving her for Debbie, she had managed to not cry, at least not until he'd left. But now she didn't seem capable of controlling her tears.

Lawrence took a handkerchief out of his pocket and handed it to her.

"Thank you," she said in a voice so timid, she hardly recognised herself.

Lawrence waited patiently for her to gather herself. When the tears had subsided somewhat she found that the knot of dread she had been carrying since leaving Tamsin's had uncoiled itself a little. As if her tears needed to come out before she could properly talk.

"The rumour is false," Diane started. "*Now*. But it was true only an hour ago." She sighed. "I've just come from Tamsin's. I broke it off after hearing what was being said about me."

"Are you in love with her? Does she make you happy?" Where Diane had been expecting mockery or disgust in Lawrence's eyes, she saw only kindness. The way he was looking at her now reminded her of how he used to look at her in the beginning of their marriage, when they were still friends above everything else.

"Maybe... I don't know. I think I might be," Diane replied. "And yes, she does make me happy. But it just can't be. If we lived in London, perhaps, but this is Tynebury, where everybody knows me, where my neighbours are my clients. Not to mention the fact that I'm about to be a grandmother."

"Diane," Lawrence said in a firm voice, "listen to me." He

deposited his glass on the coffee table and did the same with Diane's. He took Diane's hands in his. "I want to tell you something. It might be a bit painful to hear at first, but please bear with me." He took a deep breath.

"The first time I met Debbie, I was in a gloomy place. You and I had been living separate lives, despite being married. I felt like there was not much joy in my life. We both worked hard, got home exhausted at the end of the day, and didn't really talk to each other anymore. Part of me felt dead inside."

Diane started to interject, but Lawrence held up his hand.

"Let me finish. Please?" He smiled at her. "Then I met this young, vibrant woman. I know you dislike her, and I understand your reasons for doing so. But, just for a minute, try to put yourself in my shoes. She was exciting, she wanted to have adventures." His face lit up as he was speaking. "And I felt alive again. I had this energy inside me I thought I'd lost forever."

Diane couldn't help but smile at this. She had experienced exactly the same thing after her first kiss—and first night—with Tamsin.

"You know what I'm talking about, don't you?" Lawrence said. "I can see it on your face. Tamsin did the same for you, didn't she?"

Diane just nodded.

"I still loved and respected you, so much, but I knew that I would not be doing what was best for either one of us if we stayed married." A hint of sorrow crept into his gaze now. "I know I hurt you deeply when I said I was leaving, but I would have ended up hurting you, and myself, even more if I had stayed and continued to feel miserable. Of that I'm sure."

"You're probably right," Diane said, "even though it didn't feel like that at the time."

"My point is that sometimes you have to take that leap, make that choice to go for your own happiness, never mind what people say. I know there was a lot of gossip about me when we split up. It was all pretty stereotypical of a mid-life crisis, wasn't it? It wasn't pleasant to hear those things being said about me, to have some of my friends turn their backs on me. But understand this: all of that passes with time. And after it has passed, you're left with a relationship that makes your life richer and more fulfilled. The bad is just temporary, but the good comes out stronger."

Diane couldn't believe what she was hearing. Since their divorce, she and Lawrence had done their best to be courteous to each other, to maintain a certain dignity in the midst of all the turmoil. But they had never had an open conversation like this. Lawrence had never really opened up to her in this way.

"So you think I should go and be a lesbian?" Diane gave him a wry smile. "I should cause a scandal in the village, and the club, and not care about it? If I haven't ruined everything with Tamsin already, that is."

Lawrence laughed. "Well, I wouldn't put it like that. And I can't tell you what to do, that I've known since I first met you. But what I can do is encourage you to think about everything, and decide what's more important to you. I want the grandmother of my grandchild to be happy, to be an example of what life can be if you're true to yourself." He squeezed her hands before letting them go to pick up his glass again.

Diane's tears had dried now, but she was sure her eyes were a mess. She absolutely didn't want Debbie to see her in this state.

"I think I should go," she said, and stood. "Thank you for the talk. And please—"

"Don't worry," Lawrence interrupted her, "I'll talk to Debbie and ask her to keep this to herself. I can't tell *her* what to do, any more than I could you, but—" He paused. "She might not be your favourite person, and the feeling is quite mutual I think, but I know she will agree that this is your news to share. I also happen to know she would want you to be happy. Especially if that happiness is brought on by someone else other than me." He chuckled. "Sometimes I think she's afraid I'm going to leave her to go back to you." He shook his head.

Diane guffawed. "You're joking, surely." She stepped close to Lawrence and pulled him into a hug. "You can reassure her that there's no chance of that ever happening. I too have come to appreciate the benefits of a younger partner and could not picture myself with an old fart like you again."

"Ouch," Lawrence said, laughing.

Diane stepped out of their embrace and gave him a kiss on the cheek before walking out of the house.

CHAPTER TWENTY-EIGHT

Tamsin stared out of the window. Diane had only been gone for an hour and she missed her already. How was that even possible? They'd only been dating for ten days. A tiny blip in her lifetime. She had never thought Diane would put other people's opinions over her feelings for Tamsin, but that was exactly what was happening. Tamsin snorted softly. She should be relieved Diane had left, instead of feeling like this. Or so she'd like to make herself believe.

She did the only thing she could do when she felt like this. Call Eve.

"Please tell me you're calling to say you're joining me at dad's," Eve said as soon as she picked up. "Do you have any idea what that man likes to do of an evening for sheer excitement?" A loud sigh came through the receiver. "Sit in his favourite chair and stare out of the window. We're talking stationary birdwatching here, Taz. He's driving me mad."

The thought of running away to Derbyshire was very appealing, but Tamsin had clients to consider. The reason why she wasn't able to join her sister in the first place hadn't changed. "Sorry, sis," she said.

"Oh." Eve went silent. "What's going on? You sound a bit dour."

That was the magic of talking to her sister. Tamsin didn't even have to say anything. Even over the phone, with only a tinny audio connection between them, Eve could tell something was wrong. "Diane," was all Tamsin managed to say.

"What about Diane?"

"I think she left me." A pang of sorrow shot through her chest.

"What happened?" Eve asked. "Hold on, Tazzie. I'm just going to take this outside."

Tamsin pictured their father's house, the messy chaos in which he always claimed to find exactly what he was looking for. The small windows he loved peering out of.

"She overheard someone talking about us. Apparently someone saw me leaving her house early in the morning and the village tongues have started wagging."

"To be expected," Eve said matter-of-factly.

"It made her fall apart right in front of me," Tamsin said.

"She's probably scared," Eve said.

"I'm sure she is, but is that really a good enough reason to walk out on me? To tell me she can't be with me?"

"I'm sure for her it is." Eve paused. "Her entire identity has been turned upside down. She was probably working hard to come to terms with it and then she had to deal with this gossip about her… She's not a flexible young thing like us anymore."

"I can understand that, which I told her. But she just left." And that hurt, Tamsin added in her head.

"Maybe she just needs some time."

"Maybe, but what am I meant to do with myself in the meanwhile?"

"The only thing you can do: be patient and give it to her."

"From what she said, I don't think it's just time she needs. The words she spoke sounded pretty definitive."

"They're just words, though. Spoken in the heat of a very difficult moment." A short silence fell. "Don't forget, it might be 2018, but this is still a very heteronormative world we live in."

Tamsin scoffed. "And it always will be."

"I don't believe that, but let's not have that discussion right now," Eve said. "What I'm trying to say is that Diane's adjusting. She's figuring out who she is in this world that's still the same, but in which she has so abruptly changed. We might not realise this on a conscious level, but conforming to society is a big thing in most people's lives. Especially if you've done so all your life and if you've lived in a small village like Tynebury to boot."

"What do you think I should do?" Tamsin stared out of the window. The rain kept on falling and it was the prefect embodiment of how she was feeling inside.

"First of all, you should sleep on it. Give her a little time to digest what has happened and let everything cool off. But don't leave it too long to talk to her." Eve paused again. "It might not be over, Tazzie. She'd be a fool to leave you."

"So you're saying I should be the bigger person?"

"Of course," Eve said without hesitation. "What she said might have hurt you. I'm sure it did because you're crazy about her and it's not what you wanted to hear, but you're the strong one at this point in your relationship. You know who you are. It's up to you to show her that, to say it whimsically, it's okay to be gay." Eve ended with a chuckle.

Tamsin rolled her eyes. At least her sister always managed to make her laugh, even when she was feeling dreadful.

A noise outside drew Tamsin's attention. A car was pulling into the driveway. Diane's car. Her heart started pounding in her chest. "I think she just pulled into my driveway."

"There you go," Eve said. "Us Foxleys are very hard to stay away from."

Tamsin glared at the car. The engine shut off and the lights were dimmed, but no one got out.

"What if she's only here because she forgot something," Tamsin said.

"Don't be silly. She could have picked up her forgotten knickers next week," Eve said. "And what are you still doing on the phone with me? Open the door!"

"Okay." Tamsin's pulse had picked up speed.

"And call me later. Or at the very least tomorrow," Eve said. "Good luck."

Tamsin hung up and gave it a few more seconds, but Diane still wasn't getting out of her car. She inhaled a lungful of air and walked into the hallway to open the door.

The windscreen of Diane's car was covered in raindrops so Tamsin couldn't quite make out her face, but just seeing her silhouette was enough for her heart to leap into her throat. She'd come back. Whatever that might mean.

Tamsin waited, grabbing Bramble by the collar so she wouldn't bound out into the drenched road. Finally, after another minute of tense waiting and the dull thud of raindrops on the driveway, the car door slowly opened. Diane got out and looked Tamsin in the eyes. In a matter of seconds, she was soaked through and Tamsin motioned for her to come inside.

"You'll catch your death standing there like that," Tamsin said as she opened the door wide for Diane. "Let me get you a towel."

She turned to leave, but Diane grabbed her hand. "I'll take a hug instead, if such a privilege is still available to me." She tugged Tamsin toward her.

Tamsin's resolve broke and the last sliver of anger she might still have felt fled her at the touch of Diane's hand against hers. She threw her arms around Diane and held her tightly.

"I'm sorry," Diane said, repeating the fateful words she'd

spoken earlier. "I think I had a temporary lapse into insanity, or an acute panic attack. In any case, I was a fool."

"No you weren't," Tamsin whispered in her ear. "You were just being a latebian." Diane chuckled in her embrace.

"*Your* latebian," Diane said.

"I'm so glad you came back." They broke from their hug and Tamsin took in the soaked sight of Diane. "Now let me draw you a very hot bath. You don't want to catch a cold during the tail end of tax season."

"You're such a romantic," Diane said.

"Isn't that why you came back?" Tamsin asked as she dragged Diane up the stairs.

Once Diane had slipped into the warm, foamy bath tub, Tamsin hadn't been able to resist joining her. They sat with their legs entwined in the soothing water. The white, bubbly foam rose all the way up to their chins.

"Nothing like a hot bath after you've been caught in the rain," Diane said.

"Caught?" Tamsin raised her eyebrows. "Stood around in it rather foolishly, I would say."

Diane locked her gaze on Tamsin's. "I went to see Lawrence. I'm still not quite sure what pushed me to go to him. Can you believe that he's the one who talked sense into me?"

Tamsin shrugged. "You were once married to him. The man must possess some wisdom."

This elicited a throaty chuckle from Diane. "I was glad to find out that at least a little bit of his brain has remained inside his skull after his mid-life crisis."

"How did he react?"

"He was surprisingly calm, actually." Diane pursed her lips. "Perhaps even weirdly calm and supportive. Not at all how I would react if he told me he was leaving Debbie for a man." She broke out into a right old giggle.

"How would you react to that?" Tamsin asked, as a joke.

"Impossible to say, but thanks for putting that image in my head."

"You brought it up. Anyway, what's wrong with that? You expect the village to accept you, yet you're put off by the image of your ex-husband with another man? That's just plain hypocrisy."

"Stop it, please." Diane wiggled her toe against Tamsin's calf in the water. "Have mercy."

"I'm sure Lawrence has no problems picturing the two of us together." Tamsin wasn't ready to surrender just yet.

"If this is your way of making me pay for walking out on you, it's working." Diane covered Tamsin's knees with her hands. "I'm sorry for my reaction. You were right, I was spinning out of control. Now that I've had some time to consider things, I couldn't care less about what Debbie—or the rest of the world for that matter—thinks of me."

"You're going through all the stages at lightning speed, like a true lesbian. When are you moving in?" Tamsin laughed at her own joke. When she looked at Diane, she found her staring back with a blank expression on her face.

"I know you're a catch, Tamsin Foxley." Despite the relaxed atmosphere, Diane sounded serious. "I can't promise to always react in the right way and there will be some difficult moments ahead, but I want to be with you. More than anything."

"Good, because I have plans for you." Tamsin ran a finger over Diane's shin.

"Seriously, Tamsin." Diane sat up, the water cascading off her shoulders. "All joking aside, I need you to know how truly sorry I am for my irrational outburst."

"I do know. This is all new to you. I don't expect you to not have a wobble from time to time. It's perfectly normal." She cocked her head. "For a woman your age."

"You'll regret saying that." Diane scooted closer and hooked her legs around Tamsin's. Water sloshed over the side of the tub but neither of them cared. Diane found Tamsin's lips and they lost themselves in a kiss. When they broke apart, Diane looked at her with a much more solemn expression than Tamsin had expected after a kiss like that.

"I'm going to have to tell Timothy next," she said.

"You don't have to come out to everyone at once," Tamsin said. "You can do it on your own terms and in your own time."

"I feel like I'd be lying to him if I kept something this important from him."

"Only you can decide when to tell the people you love," Tamsin said.

Diane nodded, then leaned in again. Before she pressed her lips to Tamsin's again, she said, "I know exactly what will help me with the decision-making process."

CHAPTER TWENTY-NINE

T he streets of Finsbury Park were bustling with activity as Diane made her way from the tube station to Timothy and Lucy's flat. She had called Timothy two days earlier to ask if she could visit them on Saturday.

"You want to come up to London?" Timothy's voice had been slightly incredulous on the other end of the line. "You never do that. What's up, Mum?" He sounded worried.

"Can't I just take a trip to the city of a Saturday?" Diane didn't want to worry Timothy needlessly, but she also didn't want to have this particular conversation on the phone. She needed to witness her son's reaction in person when she gave him the news. "I haven't been to London in ages and I have a few errands to run. I thought it might be nice to take the opportunity to have lunch with my son and daughter-in-law."

So she'd taken the early train up from Crawley. Timothy had suggested they meet for brunch at some new restaurant in his neighbourhood, but Diane had asked to meet at the apartment first so she could talk to him in the safety of his home. Not that she was afraid of him throwing a tantrum in public, but this felt like a conversation better had in private.

She arrived at the apartment building and rang the bell. The door buzzed open and Diane walked up the stairs to Timothy's flat on the first floor, nerves screaming in her whole body.

"Hello, Mum." He was waiting for her in the open door to the flat.

"Darling," Diane said, taking her son in her arms for a hug. This steadied her a little. The feel of her son always had that effect on her. She took off her coat and handed it to him to dispose of. Lucy was waiting in the tiny living room, sitting at one end of the two-seater sofa that filled half the space. "Don't get up, dear," Diane said to her and bent to give her a peck on the cheek. "How's my future grandchild?"

"Your grandchild's doing great. Making me throw up every morning, but I suppose that's normal."

Diane sat next to Lucy on the sofa.

Timothy hovered over them, as if unsure how to act. "Would you like a cuppa?" he asked before walking over to the tiny open kitchen at the end of the living room and switching on the kettle.

Diane looked around the small flat. She had been here before of course, but it had been quite some time ago. Tim and Lucy mostly came down to Tynebury. "I suppose you'll be moving somewhere bigger once the baby arrives?"

"We've started looking," Lucy said before heaving a loud sigh. "It's not easy though. Everything's so ridiculously expensive. And if a place is within our budget it needs so much work to make it suitable for a child."

"You know I would be happy to help out. And so would Lawrence." The nerves were coming back in full force now and Diane thought it better to keep the conversation on safer topics than the one she had come to address. At least until her stomach had stopped doing somersaults. Some mild bribery wasn't beneath her in order to get her son on her side.

"No, Mum," Timothy said loudly as he took mugs from the

cupboard. "Thank you, but Lucy and I will figure it out ourselves." He brought over the mugs and placed them on the small table next to the sofa.

"I know you want to be completely independent and self-sufficient, Timothy. I admire that. But I also know the reality of London real-estate and I want my grandchild to have everything he or she needs." She looked at Lucy encouragingly. "Just think of it as an advance on your inheritance."

"It's very generous of you, Diane," Lucy said, looking at Timothy. "We'll think about it."

Diane detected a hint of determination in Lucy's voice. Maybe she would be able to convince Timothy that accepting some help from their parents wasn't a sign of weakness.

A silence fell. Diane racked her brain for something else to talk about. She never had problems coming up with things to discuss with her son. They had always been very open with each other about everything. But today was different. She knew Timothy suspected something was going on that had prompted this visit, but it was up to her to bring it up.

"How's work, darling? I've been rather busy myself, what with the end of the fiscal year. I went in to the office every day this week, can you believe that?"

Timothy brought over a pot of tea and poured it. He handed a mug to Lucy and then to Diane, before sitting down on a chair.

"Work is great, Mum." Timothy cocked his head. "You, however, seem a bit off. Is something going on?"

Diane shifted in her seat. The tea shook slightly in her hand so she put it down. "You've always been such a perceptive lad." She looked at Lucy. "Ever since he was a young boy, he could always tell when something was bothering me."

"I know what you mean," Lucy answered. "That's why I love him."

This simple phrase seemed to provide Diane with the

courage she needed. She straightened her back, turning her head towards her son again. She cleared her throat.

"You're right that there's something on my mind," Diane started, "something I need to talk to you about. I'm not really sure how to go about it, because it's not something I had ever thought I would have to talk about with you. I suppose I'm just afraid of how you'll react." She stopped, unsure of how to continue.

"You're kind of scaring me now," Timothy said. "Is it your health? Is something going on?"

"No, love, it's nothing to do with my health." Diane paused. "Or maybe it is to do with my health, my mental health." She cleared her throat. "I've been quite... sad ever since the divorce from your father. I didn't realise just how sad I was myself, really, until recently. Because you see, I've been feeling quite the opposite for the past couple of weeks." She took a deep breath. "I've been seeing someone. Romantically, I mean."

She scanned Timothy's face, waiting for his reaction. It took him a second, but soon enough his mouth started spreading into a smile.

"That's wonderful. I've been telling you for ages you should try to find someone new."

"That you have. What I'm unsure about is how you'll react when I tell you who it is I'm seeing." Her glance skittered away from him now. This was the crucial part of her announcement.

"Hold on," Timothy said. Diane's gaze went back to him and saw him frown. "It's not Lionel, is it?"

A laugh bubbled up from deep inside Diane and took away some of the tension that had been building in her gut. "No, dear," she said. "I haven't been *that* desperate." Diane steeled herself to take the final step in the process she had set in motion by coming up to London. "It's Tamsin, the new golf pro at the club." There, she'd said it.

Timothy's eyes opened as wide as Diane had ever seen them

and his mouth seemed to fall open a little. Diane heard Lucy take in a breath. Neither of them said a word.

Diane's heart sank. Maybe her son wasn't ready for this. Maybe she should have waited.

"B—but," Timothy finally said. "I don't understand. Tamsin is a woman. You, er, you're…" Confusion was clear on his face. "But you're not gay, are you? You were married to Dad for so long. So how can you be seeing this woman?"

Diane tried to put on her most reassuring smile. She found herself calmer now that she'd told Timothy. As if saying it to him out loud had lifted the burden of worry she'd been carrying around.

"I don't know if I would call myself gay. I don't know if I would call myself anything, really. It's all so new to me as well." She chuckled. "Tamsin has been calling me a latebian, which I suppose is an accurate description."

Timothy didn't look amused at this. "Who is this Tamsin, anyway? She's much younger than you, isn't she? How do you know she's not some gold digger, seducing you to get to your money?" He shook his head.

"Timothy," Diane said in a firm tone now. "I may be older than she is, but I still have all my faculties and I think I would be able to see through that kind of ploy, if that were the case. But it's not. We're in love." She felt herself go all mushy inside. "She makes me happy."

Diane felt Lucy's hand on her arm. "I'm happy for you, Diane. You deserve to have someone in your life who makes you feel like that." Lucy turned to Timothy and said in an authoritative tone, "Whoever that person is."

Lucy's words seemed to shut Timothy up for a moment, but his face still betrayed his dismay. "But—" he started.

"I understand this is a lot to take in." Diane stood. "I need to use the loo, so please take these few minutes to absorb the news." She walked out of the living room, through the corridor, to the bathroom. She didn't really need the loo, but a few minutes on her own to collect herself. And she wanted to give Timothy some privacy as well. She lowered the lid of the toilet and sat.

His reaction was certainly not what she had hoped for. Nevertheless, she felt much lighter than before she'd arrived. It was out in the open now, too late to take it back. She had just come out to her son, the first step in what she expected would be a continuous journey if things continued to go well with Tamsin.

Diane thought about the other night, her dramatic departure from Tamsin's cottage and her return to it not long after. About the feeling of coming home that had overwhelmed her when Tamsin had pulled her into her arms, still dripping wet from the rain. And that feeling told her that, even if her son needed some time to adjust to the situation, she had made the right choice.

She pulled the flush and opened the door. She heard Lucy's voice coming from the living room.

"You will support her and be happy for her." Diane stood still in the corridor. It was clear her daughter-in-law was not afraid of laying down the law. "Our child will grow up seeing there are all kinds of love in the world and knowing its grandmother is a happy woman because of that." Diane's heart grew a few sizes at this. At least she was sure her son had made the right choice of partner for himself.

She walked back into the living room and took in the scene. Lucy and Timothy were standing next to the sofa, holding hands, their heads close together. Diane gave a small cough and they both turned towards her.

Timothy let go of Lucy's hand and stood in front of Diane. He cleared his throat.

"Mum, I'm sorry about my reaction. It's just—you took me completely by surprise."

Diane brought her hand up to his cheek. "That's all right, darling. I understand you're in shock. I'm still a bit in shock myself. You can take all the time you need to get used to the idea. And when you're ready, I would love for you and Lucy to come down to Tynebury to meet Tamsin. I'm sure you'll love her." A wave of emotion swelled up inside Diane at the thought of introducing the two people who mattered most to her.

"Well," Timothy said, a smile on his face now, "if I was able to tolerate Debbie, I'm sure I can grow to like Tamsin as well." He grinned at Diane now. "I'm hoping for some free lessons for our child once he or she is old enough to hold a golf club."

Diane pulled her son into a tight hug. "I'm sure we can arrange that," she said, tears of joy gathering in the corner of her eyes. She held him for several seconds, until he started to squirm, just like he used to when he was a boy.

CHAPTER THIRTY

Tamsin's father wasn't a man of many words at the best of times, but he was being especially quiet today. He usually loved being surrounded by his daughters and son-in-law, Tamsin knew, but today he seemed a little ill at ease. No wonder, Tamsin thought, as she looked over at Diane, who sat across from her.

"William Foxley, birdwatcher first, wood worker second, father third," Eve said. "That's what I'm going to put on your gravestone."

Tamsin witnessed how Diane's eyes widened. She clearly wasn't used to Eve's indelicate ways yet. For most, it was an acquired taste—one James had acquired a long time ago, because he burst out into laughter.

"You know Dad will outlive us all," Tamsin said. "There's no point waiting for our inheritance because we'll never actually get our hands on it." Tamsin wondered if she had sufficiently warned Diane about how the Foxleys could have a go at each other when united. Their mother had been the worst of all, turning affectionate teasing into a sport, and these days, they engaged in this sort of banter not only because it was their way, but also to keep her memory alive.

"It'll all go to the Derbyshire Birdwatching Society, no doubt," Eve said. "They need it more than us, I guess."

"Diane," their father said. "I hope you'll do a better job with Tazzie than James has done with Eve." He sighed. "Do I look like a man who deserves this kind of blatant disrespect from his own offspring?"

"You most certainly do not, William," Diane said. "But alas, I can't make you any promises, except that I'll do my best to teach your girl some respect." She shrugged. "It doesn't seem to have worked so far."

"As the older generation, it's our duty, you know," Tamsin's father said. "I suppose I've failed miserably, although I've made a habit of blaming their mother. As she's no longer around to defend herself, it's rather easy."

Actually, Tamsin thought, her mum and dad matched each other in the dark humour department. That was one of the best memories she had of the two of them together when she was a child: her mum and dad howling with laughter at something Tamsin was too young to understand.

"So," her father took a sip of his wine as he regarded Diane. Tamsin thought he looked more at ease—probably because he had assessed that Diane could take a joke. Here we go, she thought, because Tamsin knew this was only the beginning. "If a man were to want his books cooked, you'd be the person he'd call?" he asked with a deadpan expression on his face. It was all in the delivery with her dad.

"Dad, come on," Tamsin protested.

"I do have my inheritance to the Derbyshire Birdwatching Society to consider, Tazzie," her dad said. "I don't want to leave its esteemed members hanging."

Tamsin shook her head. She found Diane's gaze and mouthed 'Sorry'. Diane grinned at her.

"I can't promise to cook your books, William," she said. "But next time, come around to my house, and I'll cook you a nice roast."

"Hm, very well," her dad said. Tamsin could tell the next impoliteness was already brewing in his mind. If he was on a roll, like Eve, the man was relentless. "The other day I read in the paper that somewhere in California a cougar killed a mountain biker. One of your kind that was, I gather. Please know that Tamsin has family members who'd like to keep her around a while and refrain from tearing her insides out with your fangs." He still had the same deadpan expression on his face.

"Dad," Eve said between hiccups of laughter. "You're so bad." She was sitting next to Diane and put a hand on her shoulder. "Feel free to tell him to keep his gob shut if he goes too far. Not that I can promise it will work."

"Don't worry too much, though," James said. "When I first met Eve, I thought she was the sweetest, most delightful girl. Until I got to know her better *and* was introduced to her family. You'll get used to it." He held out his glass across the table for Diane to clink hers against.

"There's no way you ever thought of Eve as sweet," Tamsin said.

"I hope not," Eve said. "Our entire marriage would be based on a lie. I don't want to be married to someone who considers me *sweet*."

"All right, all right," James said. "I clearly misspoke. I thought you were positively draconian, darling. A formidable beast of a woman. It was love at first sight."

Tamsin had often wondered how they got any eating done when they dined together as a family, between the peals of laughter and the inevitable desire to outdo each other, especially between her and Eve. She glanced at the empty chair at the head of the table, where her mother would have sat. She wished she could have introduced Diane to her mum, but this was the family she had left, and Diane was part of that now—if anything, the relentless teasing of her proved that.

"Do you know that all this time Tazzie said she was a lesbian I just had to take her word for it," their father said. "Because she never introduced me to anyone. I had to wait until she was almost forty to finally see it for myself." This time, Tamsin's dad held up his glass. "You seem very sweet and delightful, Diane," he said, because the man was incapable of not cracking a joke, even when he was trying to show genuine emotion—or perhaps even more so then.

But this was what Tamsin knew and a warm glow descended on her chest. They all held up their glasses and, as she drank her wine, Tamsin looked into Diane's eyes. They were dark and sparkling and from the way she looked back at her, Tamsin knew she'd get along just fine with the other Foxleys.

———

Tamsin rubbed her palms against her trousers. Then she rang the bell. As though he'd been waiting on the other side of the door, Stephen swung it open.

"Ha, Miss Foxley." He extended his hand. Tamsin shook it and followed him inside. She'd asked him to call her by her first name too many times to repeat it again now.

Stephen ushered her into his living room. "Do sit down, please." He reminded Tamsin of a teacher she'd had in elementary school—Mr Berry, a very formal, yet kind man who seemed to know everything. For the purpose of her visit, she decided to imagine it was her former teacher sitting across from her instead of her employer. "Can I offer you a refreshment?"

"Whatever you're having," Tamsin said.

"I'm having tea," Stephen said. "But I don't mind pouring you something stronger."

"Tea will do just fine," Tamsin said, regretting her words immediately. While Stephen went to get the tea she took a couple of deep breaths to steady her nerves. She told herself this was a fairly inconsequential conversation, at least in the grand scheme of things. She was only here out of courtesy—and because, from painful experience, she knew how these things could spiral out of control if she didn't get ahead of them. Telling the Royal Tynebury Golf Club's president about her relationship with one of its members was the only way for Tamsin to do this.

She had discussed it with Diane, who had been apprehensive, but once Tamsin had reminded her what had happened at her previous club, Diane had come around. Now that word was out, it would be best to get it all out into the open as soon as possible.

On the phone with Eve, she had railed against having to go through this process at all, because surely she wouldn't need to come out to the president if she'd struck up a relationship with a male member of the club, but this was simply how things stood. Tamsin might be out and proud, but the very fact of even having to call it that was proof that true equality was still light years away—and would, perhaps, always be an illusion.

Anyone who deviated from the norm only a fraction had to go through a myriad of tiny humiliations and degradations in their daily life, she had said into the phone. As usual, Eve had listened patiently and then, also as usual, had said, "Just grin and bear it, Tazzie. You'll survive." Eve reminded Tamsin so much of their mother when she said things in a dry tone like that.

Stephen emerged from the kitchen with a tray in his hands. He made quick work of pouring them each a cup. He sat in a well-worn club chair with its back to the window, slung one leg over the other, and said, "What can I do for you, Miss Foxley."

"Well, Mr Bradshaw"—she thought it better to address him formally as well for the occasion—"I feel as though I need to tell you something about myself." When she'd interviewed for the position of pro at the club, the reason why she'd left her former club had never been mentioned. To say things like that out loud was not the way things were done—and was certainly not how you landed a job at a bastion of conservatism like a golf club.

Stephen drew up his eyebrows and took a sip from his tea. He gave the slightest of nods. The whole setting made Tamsin feel as though she'd been sent to the headmaster's office for inappropriate behaviour, even though she'd come here of her own volition—and she hadn't done anything wrong.

Tamsin pushed a strand of stray hair behind her ear. There really was no point beating about the bush. She had no idea how Stephen would react. "The thing is, Mr Bradshaw, I'm here to tell you that I've become romantically involved with a member of the club."

Stephen waved off her statement instantly. "I really don't see how that's any of my business. In fact, the contract of employment you have with the club forbids me to even inquire about your private life."

"That may be so, but, um, I wanted to inform you anyway. The person I'm involved with is... a woman, you see. Diane Thompson, to be exact."

Stephen sat up a little straighter and put his cup and saucer down. "Even so," he muttered, visibly flustered, "it's still none of my business."

"The reason why I came here to tell you this is because I had trouble with a similar situation at Chalstone. The circumstances were very different, but I'd much rather be totally open about it this time around." This morning, after she'd slept on the matter, Diane had, very surprisingly, offered to accompany Tamsin when she went to see Stephen. But this was something Tamsin needed to do on her own. Plus, the two of them waltzing into the president's home, with the unmistakable energy between them, would only put his hackles up.

"Well," he said, then went silent for a moment. "In that case, I must thank you for informing me." He rubbed a finger over the thin stubble on his chin.

"There will undoubtedly be rumours," Tamsin said. "Perhaps you've caught wind of them already. Either way, I thought you should know and that you should hear it from me."

Stephen nodded. "Just so you know, we didn't reject Matthew Hawkes' membership application because he's, um, a homosexual." He lifted his finger. "I can see how it could be construed that way, but the fact of the matter was that we simply couldn't admit any more new members. The sport of golf is on the up, as you know, and we had so many applications."

"I'm sure the admission board had its reasons." Tamsin wasn't so sure Stephen was being entirely truthful, but she appreciated the gesture.

"If he applies again next season, he'll be first on the list." His finger kept wagging, as though he very much had a point to prove.

The contrast with when she'd found herself in her former club's president's living room couldn't be greater. Stephen wasn't exactly jumping for joy at the news, but he simply wasn't the kind to jump for anything. Of course, Tamsin had no way of knowing how he really felt about it, but that was, in the end, none of her concern.

"I love working at the RTGC," she said. "I hope to be a part of the team for a very long time to come."

"I see no reason why you shouldn't, Miss Foxley."

Tamsin took another hasty sip from her tea, then made to get up. "I won't disturb you any longer," she said.

Stephen pushed himself out of his chair. "Very well." He walked her to the door and, before he closed it behind her, he said, "Any rumours you might hear about this won't come from me. You can be sure about that."

Tamsin nodded, shook his hand again, and headed to Diane's.

CHAPTER THIRTY-ONE

D iane stood in front of the mirror in her bedroom, brushing her hair. She'd had it cut the day before and it was looking exactly how she wanted it: not overly blow-dried, but still elegantly styled.

She put down the brush and inspected her face. A little mascara and a light layer of lip gloss were what she needed, nothing more.

As she was applying the make-up Tamsin came to stand behind her and put her arms around Diane's waist. "You look gorgeous," she said, before kissing Diane's neck. "I don't think we can go out; you look way too ravishing to not take advantage of."

Tamsin's kisses were igniting a fire in Diane's belly. She had clearly figured out Diane's most sensitive spots by now. Diane looked at Tamsin's reflection in the mirror. "Stop it right now, or we really won't make it out." She tried to extricate herself from Tamsin's arms, but Tamsin only pulled her closer.

She stopped her kisses and looked into Diane's eyes in the reflection of the mirror. "I'm very proud of you for doing this."

"I know," Diane said. "I'm quite proud of myself. Or at least

I will be, once this whole ordeal is over." An inkling of doubt started creeping into her mind. She knew she was about to do what needed to be done, but it was still daunting.

Diane and Tamsin had decided that the prize-giving ceremony for the Captain's Prize would be the perfect opportunity for them to come out as a couple. It was one of the season's most popular competitions and most members of the club would be present. Anyone who hadn't yet heard the rumours, would know about them after tonight and everything would be out in the open.

"I'm sure it won't be as much of an ordeal as you think." Tamsin put her hands on Diane's shoulders and swivelled her around so she faced her. "Isabelle will be there to support you, and Lawrence as well." She bowed her head slightly until her forehead touched Diane's. "Most importantly, I'll be there, right next to you."

The doubts Diane had experienced faded away into the background at the touch of Tamsin's skin against hers. They would get through this together.

Tamsin moved her head back and straightened her spine. "I've heard this helps to give you confidence before a momentous occasion." She put her hands on her hips, moved her shoulders back and her chest forward.

Diane giggled. "The superhero pose? Is it working?"

"Try it," Tamsin encouraged her.

Diane mimicked Tamsin's pose, closing her eyes, taking in a deep breath and releasing it slowly. "I feel empowered already," she joked.

They stood like that for a few seconds. Diane had to admit she did feel more confidence building within her. She opened her eyes to find Tamsin looking at her. Her gaze was full of love.

"You look phenomenal. Like nothing or no one can stop you." She took Diane's hands in hers. "Ready?"

Diane nodded. "Ready."

———

The drive from Diane's house to the club had been mostly silent. Diane was lost in thought, imagining the possible scenarios that could play out when people at the very traditional Royal Tynebury Golf Club realised one of their oldest members was now in a same-sex relationship. She was sure some of them would be happy, and some would disapprove, but she found that the more she thought about it, the less other people's opinions seemed to matter.

She glanced sideways at Tamsin, who was manoeuvring the car through the narrow gate of the club grounds. *She* was what mattered to Diane now. And the love they had discovered between them.

The car park was almost full and Tamsin parked the car in the closest spot she could find to the clubhouse. They both stepped out of the car and started walking up the tree-lined driveway towards the entrance to the clubhouse. The weather had finally cleared after a week of almost constant rain so they didn't need to bother with umbrellas.

Diane's hand brushed lightly against Tamsin's. Diane felt Tamsin start to grip her hand, but then release it almost immediately. She was clearly leaving it up to Diane how they would present themselves to the people they were about to face.

Diane, in turn, took hold of Tamsin's hand and intertwined their fingers. She looked at Tamsin and gave her a smile. "Better to show than tell." She lifted their hands and placed a kiss on the back of Tamsin's.

As they stepped through the automatic doors of the clubhouse, the first person they encountered was Barbara, who was hanging her coat in the cloakroom. Diane gripped Tamsin's hand a little tighter. This was it. Their first introduction as a couple.

"Hello Diane," she said. "And Tamsin, lovely to see you." She gave them both a kiss on the cheek. "How are you both?" As she said this, her glance dropped down and she saw their hands.

Her forehead creased into a frown and she looked back up at Diane. "Er, what's this then?" Her tone was not accusatory, merely inquisitive.

Diane smiled at her. "Tamsin and I... well, we've been seeing each other for a little while now."

Barbara's face turned from frowning to slightly bewildered. "*Seeing* each other," she said. She looked back down at their hands and then up again at both their faces. "Well, that's, er—"

"Darlings," Isabelle's voice boomed from behind Diane.

Diane turned around and greeted her friend with a kiss on both cheeks.

Isabelle pushed herself in between Diane and Tamsin and wrapped her arms around both their shoulders, all three of them facing Barbara now.

"Barbara," she said with amusement in her voice, "you look a bit overwhelmed. Don't tell me it's because of these two being an item."

"N—no, w—well, er, I'm not," Barbara stuttered.

Diane felt a bit sorry for her. "It's all right to be shocked, Barbara. I understand this must be quite unexpected for you. Trust me, it was a revelation to me as well." She saw how Barbara's face started to settle back into its normal expression.

"Please excuse my reaction, Diane," Barbara said. "You took me by surprise, that's all. I am, of course, delighted for you." She even gave a small smile, which was quite unusual for her.

Isabelle started to nudge Diane and Tamsin towards the door that led into the function area. "We'll talk to you later, Babs," she said. "These two ladies have a lot more people to speak to." She stopped their movement and turned her head towards Barbara again. "And Barbara, if Diane can catch a hot young lady like Tamsin, maybe there's one out there for you too." She gave a cackle and promptly walked them into the bar before Diane could see Barbara's reaction to Isabelle's jibe. Diane was pretty sure she would not be amused.

"I think I need a drink," Diane said when they were inside the bar.

Isabelle finally let her arms fall from Diane's and Tamsin's shoulders. "Let me get them, dear. Gin and tonic?"

Diane nodded.

"White wine for me," Tamsin said when Isabelle looked at her.

As Isabelle walked over to the bar to order the drinks, Diane scanned the large crowd that had already gathered. She knew most of the people who were there. She thought she detected some strange looks, but mostly people just acknowledged her presence with a small nod or smile.

Maggie was in conversation with the president but was clearly not that enthralled by what he had to say. Diane saw her look around, probably for an excuse to extricate herself. When she spotted Diane, she gave her a small wave. She said something to the president and then immediately came over to Diane and Tamsin.

Tamsin had taken hold of Diane's hand again and was softly caressing it with her thumb. She leaned over to Diane's ear and whispered, "You're doing great."

Maggie greeted them both warmly. "I heard a rumour the other day, and now I can see that, unlike most of the gossip that circulates around here, it was based on fact." She held up her hands to her face in a gesture of surprise—or was it delight? "This is great news," she exclaimed. "We've all been hoping you would find someone new to share your life with, Diane. And now look at you. You're singlehandedly dashing the hopes of all the club's bachelors." She addressed Tamsin now. "I've heard a few of them proclaim they were planning on asking you out." She laughed. "I'll look forward to their reactions this evening when they see you two."

Diane could hug her friend for being so supportive. "Thank you, Maggie."

Isabelle arrived, carrying their drinks. "Word of warning, my dears, you're the talk of the evening." She nodded her head back towards the bar. "At least three people accosted me while I was waiting to be served, asking if it was true."

Diane felt a small pang of anxiety. "What did you tell them?"

"I said it was true, and if they had a problem with it, they would have to deal with me." Isabelle gave her a wicked grin.

"I knew I could count on you," Diane said.

As she looked at her friend, Diane saw someone was waving at her from a few feet behind Isabelle. Lawrence. He was smiling widely at her and gave her a thumbs up.

Diane mouthed "Thank you," at him.

He gave a small nod and turned back to the person he was talking with. Diane saw Debbie standing beside Lawrence, looking at her. She too smiled at Diane, and for the first time it looked like a genuine sign of friendliness. Diane doubted they would ever be friends, but maybe a more amiable entente with her ex's new wife could be a positive consequence of her relationship with Tamsin.

Tamsin was in conversation with Isabelle and Maggie about how difficult the rough was these days and as Diane looked at her, listening intently and engaging with her friends so easily, she was overwhelmed with a sense of peace and wellbeing.

Everything would be all right.

A WORD FROM THE AUTHORS

After working together on publishing Harper Bliss books for several years, the next logical step could only be to actually write a book together. Harper's first co-writing experience (with Clare Lydon) had been a resounding success, so this one should be even better, no?

Turns out, it's easier to co-write with someone you don't share a home with—and are not married to.

It would be a slight understatement to say that getting to the end of the first draft of this book was a struggle. From disagreements on whether to make it a sweet or steamy romance, to discussions on which one of us is more long-winded... there were many points of contention. And when you think of the difference in writing experience between us, it's a miracle we managed it at all.

However, from the moment we announced our plan of writing this book together, we received nothing but support. From our family, our friends, Harper Bliss readers, and anyone we told about it, basically. This support is what helped us pull it off in the end. For that, we're immensely grateful.

This book would not be what it is without the stellar

editing of our good friend Cheyenne Blue. She has the invaluable capacity to be firm in her editing while still managing the fragile ego of any writer (first-time or seasoned). Her funny and encouraging comments in the margins make all the cutting and rewriting infinitely more bearable.

Thank you to our beta-reader Carrie for giving us the sweetest feedback after reading the rough and unedited version of the book.

Thank you to our proofreader Claire for her relentless hunt for the last remaining typos.

Thank you to the Harper Bliss Launch Team for their enthusiasm and their support, even for a book that is not quite a regular Harper Bliss book.

And last but far from least, thank *you*, Dear Reader! All through the process of producing this book, even when we thought it might never come together, we kept reminding ourselves of how lucky we are to do what we love, and make a living from it as well. And that's all thanks to you.

Thank you.

ABOUT THE AUTHORS

Harper Bliss is the author of the *Pink Bean* series, the *High Rise* series, the *French Kissing* serial and many other lesbian romance titles. She and her wife Caroline are the founders of Ladylit Publishing and the My LesFic weekly newsletter.

Harper loves hearing from readers and you can get in touch with her here:

www.harperbliss.com
harperbliss@gmail.com